"The Only T
Common Is The Commitment We
Have To Our Jobs."

"And this," Nick said, smiling. "I want you, Marcy. In every way a man can want a woman. And what's scaring the hell out of you is that you want me just as bad. You can't walk away from it any more than I can."

"Wrong, Nick." She took a shaky breath. "In a couple of weeks you'll be back on the job, terrorizing bad guys, and I'll be off chasing more ghosts."

"And in the meantime, we pretend that we're two friends who just happen to be staying in the same house?"

She ignored his sarcasm. "Exactly."

"I'll make you one promise," he said levelly. "You'll be just as safe in my hands as you want to be."

Dear Reader,

Let's talk about summer—those wonderful months of June, July and August, when the weather warms up and Silhouette Desire stays hot.

June: Here is where you'll find another dynamite romance about the McLachlan brothers—this time Ross—by BJ James (look for more brothers later in the year!), a *Man of the Month* by Barbara Boswell, and another installment in the *Hawk's Way* series by Joan Johnston.

July: Don't look now but it's the *Red, White and Blue* heroes! These men are red-blooded, white-knight, blue-collar guys, and I know you'll love all of them! Look for the hero portrait on each and every one of these books.

August: It's a *Man of the Month* from Diana Palmer, a story from Dixie Browning and another delightful tale from Lass Small . . . and that's just a *tiny* amount of what's going on in August.

Yes, I think summer's going to be pretty terrific, and in the meantime I want to ask you all some questions. What do you think of the Desire line? Is there anything you'd particularly like to see that we don't provide? No answer is too outrageous; I *want* to hear your opinions.

So write and let me know. And yes, I really do exist! I'm not just some made-up name that goes on the bottom of these letters.

Until next month, happy reading,

Lucia Macro
Senior Editor

RITA RAINVILLE
HIGH SPIRITS

SILHOUETTE *Desire*
Published by Silhouette Books New York
America's Publisher of Contemporary Romance

SILHOUETTE BOOKS
300 East 42nd St., New York, N.Y. 10017

HIGH SPIRITS

Copyright © 1993 by Rita Rainville

ISBN: 0-373-05792-X

First Silhouette Books printing June 1993

Printed in the U.S.A.

Books by Rita Rainville

Silhouette Desire

A Touch of Class #495
Paid in Full #639
High Spirits #792

Silhouette Books

Silhouette Christmas Stories 1990
"Lights Out!"

Silhouette Romance

Challenge the Devil #313
McCade's Woman #346
Lady Moonlight #370
Written on the Wind #400
The Perfect Touch #418
The Glorious Quest #448
Family Affair #478
It Takes a Thief #502
Gentle Persuasion #535
Never Love a Cowboy #556
Valley of Rainbows #598
No Way To Treat a Lady #663
Never on Sundae #706
One Moment of Magic #746
Arc of the Arrow #832
Alone at Last #873

*Aunt Tillie stories

RITA RAINVILLE

has been a favorite with romance readers since the publication of her first book, *Challenge the Devil,* in 1984. More recently, she won the Romance Writers of America Golden Medallion Award for *It Takes a Thief.*

Rita has always been in love with books—especially romances. In fact, because reading has always been such an important part of her life, she has become a literacy volunteer and now teaches reading to those who have yet to discover the pleasure of a good book.

To Janet Howard and Patty Cogburn—
first my readers, now my friends.
Someday, we will meet.

One

By the time Marcy O'Bannon realized she was in trouble, it was too late.

Far too late to ask questions.

And way too late to scream.

Only seconds earlier she had been standing before Cristobel Jones's front door, muttering darkly at the new, shiny key that refused to enter the equally new, shiny brass lock. The key that Cristobel had mailed to her along with the irresistible invitation to visit and track down a ghost.

It was a good thing that her spritely old friend wasn't blessed with a clutch of nosy neighbors, she'd reflected, giving the knob another frustrated jiggle. Of course, Joshua Junction, population 273, just north of the California-Mexico border, was hardly a thriving metropolis with an active neighborhood watch. All the same, two in the morning was no time to be mistaken for a burglar. When the lock finally gave a soft snick, she'd grinned triumphantly, nudged the door open and stepped into the dark room.

And that's when all hell broke loose.

A large hand wrapped around her wrist like a manacle, yanking her forward, propelling her toward the center of Cristobel's spacious living room. Another cupped her mouth, muffling her startled cry.

Marcy didn't go willingly—at least not at first. Then, armed only with fear—and a hazy idea that martial arts were based on balance and speed—she lunged forward. When she swung around, she was a fighting machine of teeth, claws and flailing feet.

With typical O'Bannon tenacity, she dug her nails into the hand grasping her wrist and aimed several frantic kicks at whatever target presented itself. Satisfaction surged through her when her foot connected with something solid, and a succinct masculine oath hissed in her ear. She might go down, but, by God, she wouldn't go easily!

But feminine fury was no match for hard muscle and a man's raw strength. After several turbulent seconds, predictably, Marcy found herself flat on her back on Cristobel's persian rug, the man's lean body holding her there with terrifying ease.

"Mphfft!"

Adrenaline-induced fury surged through Marcy, momentarily reducing her fear. Her blistering comment, muffled by a hard palm, was directed at the hand that had released her wrist and was now making a quick, thorough survey of her body, hesitating for an instant on her breast, then working down to her bare midriff and legs. Bucking beneath the large masculine hand, she regretted that there was so much bare flesh. The white halter and shorts she'd worn for the drive through southern California's rare heat wave offered little protection from the marauding touch.

Horror flared through Marcy when warm fingers brushed her inner thigh. Then, even as she instinctively made another attempt to bite the hand covering her mouth, she realized that his touch was oddly matter-of-fact. But the cold voice of reason reminded her that life never promised a happy ending. The fact that she had reached the age of twenty-seven untouched by violence or tragedy did not guarantee that things couldn't change—possibly within the next few seconds. She shivered and kicked again when the hand slid down to her knee.

"Not this time, spitfire," her captor muttered, trapping her legs with one of his own. "Settle down."

Infuriated by the thread of amusement in the deep voice, Marcy twisted and squirmed, pushing against wide shoulders. A giant was squashing her into Cristobel's expensive rug—with God only knew what intent—and his heavily muscled leg angled across hers as he advised her to settle down. And—if his tone of voice was any indication—he had the gall to think the whole thing was entertaining.

Marcy gave one last ineffective shove before flexing her fingers tentatively on his shoulders, her senses belatedly catching up with her thoughts.

Yes, indeed, he was a big man.

What's more, he was a *naked*, big man.

A tough, *dangerous*, naked, big man.

Another wave of fear swept over her. Good Lord, she wondered frantically, peering at the dark form above her, what kind of mess had she fallen into *this* time? She was just supposed to be hunting a ghost—not fighting for her life in a pitch-black room. Grisly images, the product of adrenaline and an overactive imagination, were pushing her into outright panic when the man reached up and switched on the table lamp.

Marcy drew in a ragged breath. Blinking in the sudden
blaze of light, she slid a quick glance over him, starting at
his wide shoulders and working down to his bare feet.
Well, not entirely naked, she realized with relief as he
rolled off her and sat up. Sprawling back against the
couch, his legs took up an inordinate amount of floor
space. He was wearing a pair of old and battered cutoffs
and an elastic bandage around one knee.

He was also staring.

But he wasn't as big as he'd seemed in the dark. A little
over six feet, she estimated. Six feet of long bones and hard
muscle, and he was leaning back in an obvious attempt to
reassure her. But what small comfort she gained from the
shuttered expression on his lean, tan face was canceled by
the focused expression in his dark eyes. Momentarily distracted by the blatant masculine interest, she returned his
steady look.

"You know," he said calmly, in a deep voice that jolted
her nerve endings, "you're a lousy burglar. I think a ca-
reer change is definitely in order."

She blinked at him in astonishment. "I'm not a burglar!"

"That's a relief." He rubbed his bandaged knee and
winced. "So. Who are you and what are you doing here?"

He touched his leg as if the ache were a deep, familiar
one, she thought absently, watching him frown. Then his
question sank in. "Who am *I*?" Outrage battled with the
startled realization that she no longer felt threatened, that
in some indefinable way, without uttering a soothing word,
he had reassured her.

Outrage won. "I don't believe this. You grab me, gag
me, throw me on the floor when I walk in my friend's front
door and—" She took a deep breath and started over.
"What do you mean, who am I?"

"Which part didn't you understand?"

Marcy gave him the patented O'Bannon glare, a look guaranteed to shrivel most men.

Amusement flared in his black eyes.

The man was a thug, she decided after a long, comprehensive look that he returned with interest. His hair was straight, as dark as his eyes, and there was a lot of it. His peaked brows were black slashes against his tanned skin.

The same dark, springy hair covered his chest and arrowed down, disappearing briefly beneath the waistband of his ragged cutoffs, reappearing in a crisp dusting on his legs.

His eyes gleamed at her disapproving frown.

Yes. Definitely a thug.

Sitting up and brushing at her shorts, Marcy asked abruptly, "What are you doing here?"

He shrugged. "Keeping an eye on things." Before she could ask, he added, "I'm Nick Stoner."

"Marcy O'Bannon," she murmured automatically, ignoring both his lazy grin and interested gaze. Giving him a severe frown, she added deliberately, "Of the Santa Barbara O'Bannons. Cristobel is part of our family, and if you've hurt a hair on her head you'll answer to every single man, woman and child in the clan. Got that?"

His solemn nod contrasted sharply with his snapping eyes. "Got it."

"Where is she?"

"Alaska." While Nick rubbed his knee again, his gaze remained on her expressive face, watching surprise, bewilderment and denial flicker in her eyes.

Scrambling to her feet, Marcy edged away from him. "I don't believe you. She knew I was coming to visit. She wouldn't leave—at least, not willingly. Not without telling me."

Nick stayed right where he was, dealing with her alarm the way he always did, by keeping his voice low and his movements to a bare minimum. The lady was as gutsy as she was gorgeous, he reflected, eyeing her suspicious expression. A redhead with bewitching, go-to-hell green eyes.

She was also a walking invitation to trouble. She didn't have a shred of self-preservation in her pint-size body, he decided. What Marcy needed was a good internal alarm system—and the horse sense to listen to it. He *could* have done something to the old woman. Could be an ax murderer, for all Marcy O'Bannon of the Santa Barbara O'Bannons knew. And what was she doing? Getting the hell out of there while the getting was good? Screaming the place down? No. She was standing there in an outfit that would tempt a saint, arguing with him.

"I don't believe you," Marcy repeated stubbornly.

Nick sighed. "If you know Cristobel Jones so well, tell me what she likes more than anything in the world," he challenged. "Even more than pistachios on lime sherbet."

Marcy gave him a considering glance. So he knew about Cristobel's secret vice? The knowledge reassured her. A bit.

"Finding a bargain," she said promptly. With matchmaking a close second. Very close. In fact, that—matchmaking, not pistachios—had been the topic of their last serious discussion. It had ended with Cristobel promising, *swearing,* not to drag home any more men for Marcy.

"Bingo." Nick settled more comfortably against the couch. "Two cruise lines were having a price war, and she got an offer she couldn't refuse. Cristobel," he repeated gently, "is in Alaska."

"But—"

"She left me to watch the house."

"She wouldn't—"

"Believe me," he sighed again, "she would."

"But, who are you? I know most of the people around here and I've never—"

"I'm . . . the handyman."

She gave him such a blatant look of disbelief he almost laughed. Instead, he propped his elbows on the cushions behind him and waited to see what she'd do next.

Marcy spun on her heel and marched over to Cristobel's feminine desk, reaching for her Rolodex. Flipping through the printed cards, she muttered, "Hilda, Hilda. What the heck is her last name?"

"Blunt," Nick told her. "But she calls herself Zelda these days."

Glancing at the lounging man, Marcy stared, her gaze caught and held by his amused expression. "Zelda? Why on earth would she—" Annoyed, she broke off. "You think this whole thing is very funny, don't you?"

He shrugged. "It's been different. A loony neighbor with crystal balls and ghosts keeps things from getting dull."

Crystal balls? Frowning, Marcy picked up the receiver and poked at the buttons. Hilda, Cristobel's neighbor and close friend, was a night owl. As far as she was concerned, two in the morning was the shank of the evening, and she was as fond of talking as Cristobel was of lime sherbet.

"Hilda?" Marcy brightened. "This is Marcy. Do you know where— What? Call you Zelda?" She glared at Nick, daring him to say a word, scowling when he just widened his eyes and shrugged.

"You've changed your name? I see." She hesitated and said bluntly, "No, I don't. Why? I mean, why Zelda?

What was the matter with Hilda?'' She stared at Nick, noting his interest in her brief shorts.

"Your *what* said so? Ah.'' Her brows rose. "Your... astral guide said it wasn't an appropriate name for a psychic? I didn't know you were a—" Taking a deep breath, Marcy said, "Okay, Zelda, do you know where— What?'' She stared at Nick and repeated numbly, "The moon is in conjunction with Mercury and it's a propitious time to study her crystal ball." She almost threw the phone at him when he grinned.

"Why do you want to study a— No,'' she stopped, knowing the answer would only further muddy the waters. Explanations from Hilda—scratch that, Zelda— usually did. "Forget I asked. Do you know where Cristobel is?'' At the succinct reply, Marcy briefly closed her eyes. "Alaska,'' she repeated stoically.

Nick wasn't gloating. He didn't even seem to be listening. For a very good reason, Marcy decided, narrowing her eyes. He was studying her the way an artist studies a model, taking her in from her tumbled mane of hair to her bare toes. His journey was a leisurely one, dallying here, lingering there, and there wasn't an ounce of artist's objectivity in the scorching masculine gaze.

Marcy shifted, cursing the small, restless movement that betrayed her uneasiness. But then women with wild brick red hair and decidedly average features didn't learn much about dealing with dangerous men, she reminded herself. Naked or otherwise. And they were rarely the object of such total concentration.

Suddenly, Marcy was aware of a new tension in the room, a current emanating from Nick that was unnerving. "Zelda,'' she said baldly, "exactly who is Nick Stoner?''

Several minutes later, dazed by the elder woman's paean to glorious manhood as personified by Nick the thug, Marcy cradled the receiver. The peerless specimen of masculinity didn't even notice. He had finished his basic survey and was looking at her hair.

Rattled by his unblinking gaze, Marcy dropped into the nearest chair and corrected herself. *Looking* was an anemic word for such absolute concentration. He seemed to be absorbing her color and texture into his pores.

"So you're a cop," she said brightly, folding her arms across the front of her halter.

"Yep." He nodded. "In San Diego."

"And you saved Cristobel's life."

His gaze went from preoccupied to uncomfortable. "It was no big deal."

"I imagine Cristobel thinks it was."

"She's a little old lady," he said shortly. "And the guy was my size. It looked worse from where she stood. He didn't even have a gun."

"Just a knife," she said dryly. "And you hurt your leg while you were—"

"It's fine."

"Did he stab you?"

He looked affronted. "No."

Marcy bit back a laugh at the annoyance in his black eyes. Her amusement faded when she realized that she'd probably kicked his injured leg during the struggle. Well, if he thought she was going to apologize, he was dead wrong. Any man who dragged a woman into a dark room deserved exactly what he got. Even if he was one of the good guys. Besides, the way he'd swarmed all over her, he couldn't be hurting too much.

Still, he *was* rubbing his leg, and he *had* been injured helping Cristobel.

"Did I hurt your bad—"

"I said I'm fine," he said testily. "You did exactly what you should have done, but you should have done a lot more of it."

"Fine. Then we're even. You scared me and I kicked you." Marcy shot to her feet. "Well, fascinating as all this is, it's been a long day and I'm tired." She was also in no mood for a lecture, and he had the look of a man about to embark on one.

Nor did she have the energy to deal with the direct intensity of his gaze. She had seen similar looks in a nature film about predators. She hadn't enjoyed it then, and she didn't like it now.

Retreat was definitely in order. "It was nice of you to keep an eye on things for Cristobel," she told him as she headed for the door. "But since I'm going to be here for several weeks, I guess—"

"So will I."

Marcy stopped dead, then turned back to face him. "You'll what?"

"Be here. I promised Cristobel."

He probably stopped bad guys in their tracks with that soft, level voice, she thought uneasily. It didn't give an inch. Neither did the determination in his black eyes. A prudent person would know he meant exactly what he said and wouldn't argue with him. Unfortunately, no one had ever accused an O'Bannon of being prudent. The men were pragmatic to a fault, but successful in the business world and not above taking calculated risks. The women relied more on their intuition and had been known to take some staggering leaps of faith.

No, she decided ruefully, prudence was not an O'Bannon characteristic. And as much as she felt like a wren in a family of peacocks, she did share the family proclivity for believing that her way was . . . well, not the only way, but the right way.

It was that stubborn belief that had sustained her when she moved away from her close-knit, overwhelming, overprotective family into a small, self-contained apartment in Los Angeles and a life-style that allowed her the freedom to leave for days on end when her job called for it.

Nick's silent regard brought her back to the present. "We'll talk about it tomorrow," she promised, heading for her bedroom. Just as she reached for the doorknob, she heard his voice—still soft, still meaning exactly what he said.

"You bet we will, honey."

Marcy closed the door with a snap, flipping on the light. The first thing she saw was an envelope on her pillow with her name written in Cristobel's exuberant scrawl. Annoyed as she was, when she opened it she couldn't help smiling. Cristobel's glee rippled across the page like laughter.

Darling Marcy,

Alaska! The trip of my dreams. And they're practically giving it to me!

Forgive me for not being there. But I know you will. You always do.

I must ask a big favor. Take care of Nick for me. (Yes, dear, I remember our little talk, but this is NOT—repeat, NOT—matchmaking.) Nick rushed to rescue me from a mugger and was injured in the ensuing melee. (He tore a number of ligaments around his knee and escaped the doctor's knife by a hairbreadth). He's too modest to talk about it, but believe me, he risked his life for me. And whether he shows it or not, he's still in pain.

I persuaded him (with some difficulty) to recuperate at my place. Actually, I kidnapped him.

I went to the police station to thank him, learned that he was home ill, got his address despite rules saying I couldn't have it (people will give little, old gray-haired ladies ANYTHING), and went to visit him. I found him zonked out on pain pills, a captive in his second-story condo. (He couldn't get upstairs or down.) I persuaded his hulking partner, Jackson, to pack him in a car and deliver him to me.

By the time Nick cared where he was, he was settled in, with two women at his beck and call. (Hilda— I mean Zelda—just dotes on him.)

And she's not the only one, Marcy thought with a grin, kicking off her sandals and curling comfortably on the bed. Cristobel, who was a contemporary of Charity O'Bannon, Marcy's grandmother, had been a friend of the family for forty years or more. She was also Marcy's honorary great-aunt, and over the years the two of them had forged a friendship that had nothing at all to do with titles or age.

Cristobel, Marcy reflected, was a lady who was as affectionate as she was impulsive, and if she was running true to form, she was doing her share of doting. Childless and widowed years earlier, she had at various times taken a number of young people under her wing—with far less reason than she had with Nick.

Blinking thoughtfully, Marcy returned to the letter.

But he's a proud man and as soon as he didn't need so many pain pills, he started talking about leaving. He said he couldn't inconvenience me.

Can you believe that? The man saved my life! We finally struck a bargain: he would stay, but as soon as he was up and hobbling, he insisted on doing all the odds and ends around the house that I can't (or don't want) to do.

That was fine until the Alaska thing came up; then he said he'd go back to his place. The doctor told me that although Nick's leg looks fairly normal, he shouldn't be climbing stairs yet. Any strain on his leg could set him back for weeks and/or possibly result in surgery. So I told him (Nick, not the doctor) I didn't want to leave the house empty—especially with a ghost wandering around. He couldn't stand the sight of a pathetic, sniveling, little old woman, so he agreed. I asked him to stay—even if some of my friends dropped by. Meaning you, of course. He promised that he would, believing (I assume) that they'd have the good sense and courtesy to leave when they found I was gone.

Marcy, you MUST stay. And you MUST keep him here. I realize that it might not be easy, but I'm trusting you to carry on for me. I won't go to my grave knowing that I ruined a man's good leg.

Or a good man's leg.

Whatever. Watch over him for me.

Love, Cristobel

P.S. I promise you I'm not matchmaking. Nick wouldn't do for you at all. He doesn't believe in ghosts.

P.P.S. Ask Hilda—drat it, Zelda—about the ghost. She knows all about him. See you in a couple of weeks.

Marcy dropped the letter on the bedside table and gazed thoughtfully at the ceiling fan, mesmerized by the slowly drifting blades. What was Cristobel up to? Had she really mended her ways?

Possibly.

Or had she merely changed tactics?

Probably.

But even Cristobel couldn't have known that an innocent shopping expedition in the big city would turn into a meeting with Nick Stoner, the poker-faced, half-naked— and yes, damn it—sexy policeman.

No, but she was certainly capable of turning the situation to her advantage when it did.

Sighing, Marcy admitted that it didn't really matter. She was well and truly stuck. Never in her life had she been able to turn down a cry for help, and anyone who knew her knew it. Cristobel had lured her to Joshua Junction with a ghost, then used the one method certain to keep her there.

Nick Stoner didn't look like a man who needed help. Of any kind. From anyone. But if Cristobel wanted her to keep him here, away from the dreaded condo stairs, that's what she would do. It shouldn't be too difficult, she thought with a wry lift to her brows. From the last little assurance—or threat—he had tossed at her, it sounded as if he had resolved any former doubts and decided to honor his promise to Cristobel. He would stay—whether she liked it or not.

No matter, she told herself bracingly. She could handle it. O'Bannons were good at handling things. Probably because they'd had so much practice. The current Santa Barbara head count—including her parents, five older brothers, their wives and children—stood at thirty-three, and they all shamelessly interfered in each other's lives, offering unsolicited and usually unwanted advice.

But even the O'Bannons had their limits, and an eighteen-hour day ending with a free-for-all on the floor with a naked man was hers.

Marcy opened the dresser drawer and pulled out a man's large T-shirt that she used for a nightgown, grateful that she had left a few basic necessities on her last visit. Yes, she could definitely handle Nick the thug. But she was no fool. Now that she had made her escape, she wasn't going back through the other room, past a rumpled man who gazed at her with hungry, black eyes, just to retrieve her bag. No, she decided, flipping back the apricot comforter, it could stay right on the front porch where she had dropped it. It would survive a night in the open air.

Marcy unhooked the halter, kicked off her shorts and pulled the shirt over her head. All right, she thought, staring down at the sheet, so Nick was an unexpected complication. So he was a man filled with an edgy energy that fell just short of violence, a man simmering with a potent force that shook her right down to her pink toenails. He didn't worry her.

Not much.

What did worry her was Zelda. Zelda with the astral guide and crystal ball. Rambling, dithering Zelda—who was supposed to tell her everything about Joshua Junction's ghost.

Nick listened to the snap of the closing door and grinned. Somehow Marcy O'Bannon, of the Santa Barbara O'Bannons—whoever they were—managed to pack all of her annoyance into the crisp sound. If he was any judge, and he was, she was one ticked-off lady. Getting slowly to his feet, he winced and absently rubbed his knee.

She also packed a hell of a kick. With a little training, she could be lethal.

Limping toward the front door, he grimaced. Could be? Who was he kidding? From that gorgeous head of fiery hair right down to her slim bare feet she was a menace, even to a man reputed to be cool under fire. Hell, he thought throwing open the door and reaching for her overnighter, he had been cooler on his first drug bust than he'd been holding her sleek, little body. Even Cristobel's knife-wielding junkie hadn't jangled his nerves the way she did.

He hefted the case and locked the door, testing the dead bolt. It had been his house gift to Cristobel. That and new locks on all the windows and the other doors. She had still been fussing about them when he'd driven her to San Diego to catch her plane, earnestly explaining the inconvenience of dual locks on a single door.

Inconvenience. He shook his head in disbelief. But judging by the muttering and fumbling he'd heard earlier, it was a feeling that Marcy shared.

It figured.

Neither one of them had the foggiest idea how to take care of themselves. Babes in the woods, that's what they were. He set the case on the floor outside Marcy's door and limped into the kitchen, opening the refrigerator and pulling out a beer.

Nick scowled at the chilled bottle. It was going to be a long night. His leg was throbbing like an abscessed tooth, and he spared a thought for the pain pills he'd just tossed away. Maybe it hadn't been such a good idea.

Raising the bottle to his lips he drank deeply, then headed back to the living room. He switched off the lamp, started toward his bedroom and stopped. He wouldn't sleep if he went to bed, and staring at the ceiling was no way to get through the long, dark hours. Instead, he opened the sliding glass door and stepped outside on the covered patio.

It was sultry, more reminiscent of New Orleans than San Diego's County's highly touted near-perfect climate. Dropping into one of the padded chairs, he thought again that the furniture was a perfect example of Cristobel's zeal for bargains. It was all good stuff but nothing matched. Just like her house.

Tucked overhead in one of the surrounding trees, a mockingbird loudly trilled its evening extravaganza, over-riding the song of crickets in the moonlit night. The bird's liquid melody shifted gears every few seconds, displaying its virtuosity with staggering ease.

Nick tilted the bottle and swallowed again. The song reminded him of the woman inside. He had a hunch that she had just as many facets, and that she could move from one to another with the same bewildering speed.

She was a puzzle. An intriguing one. His hand tightened around the cold glass. A sexy one. But puzzles had only one purpose—they were to be solved. To find a solution, he needed information. What did she do? How did she live? Did she make love the way she fought—throwing herself into it headlong and damning the consequences?

His eyes darkened. He hoped so.

Was she a model? As far as he was concerned, the field should be wide open for leggy redheads with kissable mouths, but he doubted that she had the patience it required. A teacher? In sales? For the first time in a long time, his cop's instincts got him nowhere.

He didn't know why she was at Cristobel's, and tracing a path down the sweating bottle, he realized that he really didn't care.

Only one thing mattered.

Keeping her there.

He wanted Marcy O'Bannon. Under Cristobel's roof, with him. Not running away from him in her jazzy, little red car, not taking refuge with Zelda. Here. Wanted her spirit, her temper, her sleek body, her kissable lips. Wanted her silky hair sliding over his chest, down his belly and thighs. Wanted her for as long as he would be here—at least two weeks.

His gaze settled on his bandaged knee and his thoughts drifted to the day it had happened. He had been off duty, about to enter the shopping mall, when he'd seen the junkie's eyes settle on Cristobel. Off duty or not, he'd done his job.

It was a job that he wouldn't change for any other, but he had no illusions about it—it was a job that played hell with relationships, that chewed them up and spit out the pieces with monotonous regularity. It was also a job that kept him from planning beyond the next fourteen days.

But he had two weeks, and before the time was up, he'd have Marcy in his bed.

Somehow.

Two

The next morning, plugging in the coffee maker, Nick wasn't any closer to a solution. He wasn't going to leave, and he didn't know if Marcy would stay when she discovered that he'd meant what he'd said: that he'd be sharing the house with her. Too bad that handcuffing a woman and chaining her to a bedpost was frowned upon these days, he thought idly. Especially for a cop. Whistling softly, he slid his hands in the back pockets of his comfortably worn jeans and watched the coffee stream into the glass pot.

"You still here?" Marcy stood in the doorway, sliding a ribbon beneath her hair and tying it loosely at her nape. Her drowsy green eyes brightened when she spied the coffee.

Nick rocked back on his bare heels. "Still here," he agreed, eyeing her knit shirt. It was pink and clung to all the right places.

"You going to stay?"

His gaze shifted to her mouth. "Yeah."

"Even though I'm going to be here?"

"Uh-huh." Especially since she was going to be there. He lowered his gaze a few notches more. Her pink shorts were nice, too. They were as brief and clingy as the shirt and showed lots of leg.

If he had learned anything in his line of work, it was patience, so now he waited, wondering what argument she'd drum up to boot him out of the house. He was more surprised than disappointed when the speculative gleam in her eyes turned to resignation.

Instead of heaving the sigh he expected, she gave a hopeful sniff. "Is the coffee done?"

Letting out a long, silent breath, Nick took two mugs from the cupboard and set them on the counter. So Marcy O'Bannon of the Santa Barbara O'Bannons wasn't going to run. She looked more philosophical than thrilled by the prospect, but she was definitely going to stay. He didn't waste time wondering why. In fact, he was willing to bet next month's paycheck that her decision was based entirely on her friendship with Cristobel and a complicated blend of gratitude and obligation. He had a hunch that when Marcy was committed to something—as she was to Cristobel's well-being—she was definitely in for the long haul. He shrugged, silently admitting that he didn't much care why. He was just grateful that he didn't have to limp around the house playing on her sympathy and that they were staying under the same roof.

Life was looking up, he reflected, reaching for the glass pot. Way up.

The next several weeks were going to be interesting, he thought, pouring coffee into the mugs. In two brief meetings he'd already learned that Marcy was loyal and protective, brave as she was foolhardy, and needed a jolt of caffeine to jump start her in the morning. She also had a short fuse that he couldn't wait to ignite.

Among other things.

"I don't like people coming in my room when I'm asleep," Marcy said quietly, settling her pink-clad bottom on a bar stool. Her small frown lightened a fraction when he slid a mug in front of her.

He shrugged. "I thought you'd like your things when you got up."

"That was . . . kind." She carefully spooned some powdered cream into her mug before looking up at him. "I appreciate the thought, but—" her green gaze was cool and level "—I appreciate my privacy even more. I would have managed."

Nick's brows rose. Yep, she had it reined in, but the lady had a temper. Even more to the point, she was probably right. No, damn it, she *was* right. He had no business going into her room.

Not yet.

And when he did go back in, he promised himself silently, it wouldn't be mere courtesy or business that took him there.

No, last night he had acted on impulse, surprising himself as much as he would have his partner. He stopped a grin with a long swallow of coffee. He was not an impulsive man, and Jackson would be the first to agree that Nick Stoner was methodical and a bit plodding—he did things by the book. Hell, Jackson had said more than once that he *wrote* the book.

He had gone back to her room, opened the door and set the case inside, intending to leave without a look at the bed. Then she had moved, shifting the sheets with a silken murmur, and uttered a soft, drowsy sound that cut off his breath.

And, body tight and aching, he had looked.

She slept on her stomach, her cheek resting on the back of her hand, one knee slightly bent. The flowery sheet, pulled taut across the swell of her bottom, was a stark contrast to the strip of tan, satiny flesh beneath the hiked-up masculine T-shirt. With his fingers gripping the edge of the door until his knuckles had whitened, he'd wondered about the man who had given her the shirt, the man fool enough to let her go traipsing off on her own. Then, realizing he was wondering too damn much, he'd left while he could still walk away.

"You're welcome," Nick said dryly, leaning against the counter, gazing pointedly at her coffee. "And you're right. I apologize." Taking advantage of her surprise, he asked mildly, "Can you cook?"

Marcy eyed him thoughtfully, then lifted one shoulder in a slight shrug. "I fall in the category of being able to read a recipe and follow instructions. What I get is... uninspired results. But Cristobel and I have a long-standing arrangement—she cooks and I clean up." She looked at him hopefully. "How about you?"

Nick sighed. "I live alone. I like to eat. So I cook. Nothing fancy. What do you do about food when you're at home?"

Marcy shrugged again. "Depends. My hours are crazy when I'm working, and I'm on the road a good deal of the time doing research, so I eat out a lot and just keep a few things around. I heat a mean can of soup and make great sandwiches. And while I'm down here," she said patiently, as if pointing out the obvious, "I'm working. Don't expect me to turn off my computer when your stomach grumbles and whip up cozy little meals for two."

Nick wrapped his hands around the mug, zeroing in on one word. Research? "You use a computer?"

"Most writers do," she assured him absently, concentrating on her argument. "Research takes a lot of time and—"

"Books?"

"Magazine articles for now, but we're talking about food," she pointed out, keeping her priorities in order.

"You don't look like a writer."

With a sigh that said she'd heard the statement before, Marcy demanded, "What's that supposed to mean, that I don't look like a walking dictionary? I didn't expect generalizations from a cop. Just for future reference, we come in all sizes and shapes. Big, little, narrow and wide. You name it, we got it."

"I can't see you sitting still long enough to write," he said mildly, interrupting her energetic lecture.

"Oh. We're talking deductive reasoning here, not generalization."

"You got it."

Marcy shook her head. "This time, Sherlock, you're wrong. Half wrong, anyway," she amended conscientiously. "I don't like to sit for hours on end, but I do it. But we're straying again," she reminded him in a brisk tone. "We're still talking about food."

"Right." Nick mentally added a good appetite to the things he'd learned about her. "Food."

"More specifically, the fact that you cook." Looking around pointedly, she asked, "What do you cook?"

Wondering what kind of research called for pink shorts, he murmured, "Eggs?"

"Cholesterol?"

"Do we care?"

"That all depends on what the other choices are."

"Oatmeal?" He hoped to God she was as repelled by the offer as he was.

Marcy wrinkled her nose.

"Pancakes?" Before he could tell her his next offer would be a box of cereal, they were interrupted by a warbled song outside of the open window. It led to the back door and ended in a trill of delight.

"Marcy! I just knew you would be here." The screen door flew open and banged shut behind the plump woman beaming at them.

Marcy swung around, her smile faltering as she eyed the apparition standing in the doorway. All that remained of Hilda Blunt was the chirpy soprano voice. Gone were the straight gray hair and decorator glasses. No more pleated slacks and stylish blouses. In her place—apparently—was Zelda, with masses of platinum blond curls controlled by a beaded headband. Her brown eyes blinked nearsightedly and a bangled ethnic dress of indeterminate origin floated around her ankles. More than a dozen slim bracelets jangled on her arm.

"I just talked with you last night," Marcy reminded her dryly. "It couldn't have been that hard to figure out."

"Ah, but you didn't say where you were." Touching two fingers to her forehead and closing her eyes, Zelda murmured, "But...I knew. Gray Feather said I would find you."

"Who's Gray Feather?" Marcy asked blankly.

"You would ask," Nick muttered, dumping some pancake mix and milk into a bowl and stirring briskly.

"My guide." Zelda opened one eye and peered at the bowl. Apparently satisfied that Nick was making enough for her, she returned to her trance. "He said...he said..."

"Guide?"

"Guide," Nick affirmed dryly.

Marcy blinked. "What kind of guide?"

"A dead one."

Almost dropping the mug in her excitement, Marcy demanded, "You mean he's my ghost?"

"Oh, hell." Nick turned his attention from the heating skillet to glare at her. "Not you, too."

"Yep." She grinned at his weary disgust. "I'm here to dig up the dirt, if you'll pardon the expression, on the local ghost—feathers, war whoop and all. That's my job."

"He said," Zelda repeated testily, opening her eyes, "that you would be here." She focused on Marcy. "And, no, he isn't your ghost. He's my—"

"Guide," Marcy said soothingly. "Is he going to help us find the ghost?"

"That's my job, not his."

"Then, what does he do?" Marcy gave Nick an absent smile as he slid a plate of pancakes in front of her.

Zelda pulled herself up on the stool next to Marcy, picked up a fork and shot Nick a look of anticipation. "He guides me."

"Where?" Marcy asked thickly, swallowing.

Giving a wave that managed to be both airy and vague, she said, "Though my new world." Her eyes brightened when Nick handed her a steaming plate. "Sweet boy," she murmured, pouring a lazy trail of syrup over the hotcakes.

Marcy slanted a stunned look at the older woman. When she turned to look at him, Nick met her gaze and gave her a half grin, raising his dark brows in mute inquiry.

Marcy's eyes narrowed. There was nothing sweet or boyish about him, and any woman with both feet planted firmly in this world would know it. She didn't have a psychic bone in her body, but what she was picking up from the banked fires in Nick Stoner was practically singeing her nerve endings.

He was a quiet, understated man, one who didn't flaunt his masculinity. He didn't have to. Every gene in his lean body merged to sing an anthem to it. He was dark and dangerous—and, with her deadline looming, he was a distraction that she couldn't afford. For two reasons.

The first, because he didn't believe in ghosts.

And being male—at least, if he resembled her brothers and numerous cousins—he was undoubtedly convinced that since he didn't believe in ghosts, neither should she. He would waste precious time dealing with the matter in logical and pragmatic terms. And completely missing the point.

Few of the men in her family had understood her fascination with the unusual, the slightly offbeat, regarding her interest in such matters with suspicion, half convinced that she would one day slip over some tenuous line into outright weirdness. After years of dealing with their relentless pragmatism and heavy-handed interest in her affairs, moving away seemed the easiest solution. She loved each and every one of them, but they were driving her crazy. An apartment in an upscale Los Angeles neighborhood had been the solution. It was close enough to visit and far enough away to live her own life.

Oddly enough, she thought wryly, for such practical men, they had managed to overlook the most obvious fact: that she made a very nice living doing exactly what she chose to do, researching and writing about the bizarre.

And the second reason? Because Nick Stoner didn't try to hide the fact that he wanted her. His dark eyes burned with it, and the room was charged with electricity when he looked at her. Because he challenged her, scared the living daylights out of her. And because, once, in the not too distant past, a brief episode with a man very much like Nick had left her with the depressing conclusion that she was probably not the right kind of woman for a wild affair. Or possibly any type of affair. Actually, the words Jeffrey had tossed at her had been, "not enough woman."

Popping one last bite into her mouth, Marcy reminded herself for probably the thousandth time that the entire responsibility for the fiasco was not hers. Jeffrey had had a few problems of his own. But one way or another, the incident had left its mark. She was definitely treading cautiously around men these days.

Nick brought his plate over to the bar and sat next to her. "Tell me you don't really believe in ghosts," he demanded, popping a forkful of pancakes into his mouth while he waited.

"I keep an open mind," she said tactfully, sliding off the stool to refill their mugs. And to put some distance between her and Nick the thug, she admitted with silent honesty. "Especially while I'm investigating the matter. It doesn't help to go into these things with your mind already made up."

He nodded, watching her pour the coffee. When she finished, she stayed where she was, lacing her fingers around her mug. He was surprised at the tug of disappointment he felt. He wanted her closer. "You're right, it doesn't. But as one investigator to another, I'd like to know how you plan to check out a ghost."

"Bring him out of the closet?"

"Very funny."

Zelda's intent gaze slid from Nick's intent face to Marcy's. "Some of my dearest friends are spirits, especially Gray Feather," she reminded them in a troubled voice. "I won't help you if you intend to make a mockery of them."

"Good."

"That's the last thing in the world I'd do," Marcy said hastily, raising her voice to override Nick's. Glaring at him before she turned to Zelda, she added, "I've never had an experience with a spirit—good or bad. I'm coming at this from an absolutely neutral position. In fact, that's the main reason I want to do this story. I want to see for myself. The one thing I can promise is that I'll be fair. I won't turn the article into one of those sleazy tabloid things." She moved to stand directly across from where Zelda was seated.

Brown eyes examined earnest green ones. The older woman finally gave a quick little nod. "I suppose it's all right," she murmured. "Cristobel gave me copies of some of your articles. They're very good." Her eyes widened. "Who knows, maybe Gray Feather has read them." Both of the women ignored Nick's groan. "Gray Feather did tell me to find you—and he never makes mistakes," she added, beaming at Marcy.

"Tell me about the ghost." Marcy slid onto a stool at the end of the bar, as far from Nick as she could get. "What's his name? Why is he haunting Joshua Junction and what kind of haunting does he do?"

"Well," Zelda admitted reluctantly, "no one has actually *seen* a ghost—"

"Indian or otherwise," Nick said, taking the plates to the sink.

"—so I don't actually know his name."

"Come on, Zelda, admit it, you don't even know if there is a ghost."

"But, Nick, dear boy, I do know. There has to be." She turned to Marcy. "You see, exactly 100 years ago Joshua Junction was built on land that had once been an Indian village."

"What tribe?"

"A branch of the Mojaves, I think. We have a nice little museum in town where you can clear up all the fine points."

Marcy grinned. Zelda's airy gesture made it clear that she wasn't interested in historical data, and if there was grunt work to be done, it would be up to Marcy to do it. Ah, well, she reminded herself, that was one of the joys of being a writer. Research. Digging into dusty files and letters, interviewing the locals—the older the better—poking her nose into things that people often preferred to have remain buried in the past. It was, she admitted, her favorite part of the job. That and the fact that she got paid for being nosy.

"The important thing is, this is our centennial, and I think that's why the ghost has appeared."

"Sort of a belated protest against the land-grabbing white men?" Nick asked.

"I don't think so. I don't pick up any negative vibrations. Perhaps it's because there's a lot of activity involving the centennial. Whatever it is, he's making himself known."

"Wait a minute." Marcy gazed thoughtfully at the two of them. "Do we know for sure it's a he? Couldn't it be an Indian woman?"

"No." Zelda shook her head. "The emanations I pick up are definitely masculine."

"Too bad. Some of the women's magazines I write for would love it. Okay, so we have an Indian, male, over 100 years old." Marcy waited. When the older woman didn't elaborate, she prodded gently. "What else do we have? If no one has seen him, how do we know we have a ghost?"

"Because the unusual occurrences of the past six months are ghostly in nature," Zelda said patiently.

Marcy gave a gurgle of laughter. "Can you believe we're actually sitting here talking about dead people appearing as if it were the most natural thing on earth?"

"But it is." Silvery blond curls bobbed as Zelda emphasized the point with a nod. "Spirits are very active. We usually have several of them watching over us."

Nick perched on his stool again. "Us?"

"Us," Zelda said firmly. "All of us. Whether we believe it or not."

"That must keep them busy. Let's get back to the famous ghost," Nick suggested. "What unusual occurrences?"

Zelda's eyes lit up. "Misty lights, wild cries in the night, local dogs agitated and howling. All of the happenings taking place just a mile or so down the road, smack in the middle of where the old Indian village used to be."

"If I'm not mistaken, it's also where the old, abandoned Mulroony estate is, complete with a crumbling Victorian nightmare."

Marcy grinned at Nick's dry tone. "You have no romance in your soul," she assured him. "This could be the story of the year. It has everything. A Gothic mansion, ghostly lights, ghastly cries, things that go bump in the night. It's perfect! I can't wait to get started."

"I'm a realist," he said flatly, her entranced expression sending a wave of uneasiness through him. "If something's going on at the Mulroony place, my gut tells me that someone is making it happen. And I don't mean a ghost. If I had to put money on it, I'd bet on flesh-and-blood people." He took a long swallow of coffee, regarding Marcy steadily over the rim of the mug. "There could be any number of reasons they're doing it, and every one of them add up to trouble. I don't want either of you going near the place."

"Are you insane?" Marcy stared at him, amazement raising her voice a notch. "Or have you forgotten why I'm here? I'm researching a ghost, and part of the job is to go where he is. So that's exactly what I'm going to do." As a muscle flexed in his jaw, she added for good measure, "I'm good at my job and I've been at it long enough to know what I can handle. I don't need a guardian or a bodyguard telling me what I can and cannot do. So if you're in the mood to play cops and robbers, you can just do it with someone else."

With an exasperated wave of her hand, she disregarded his theory. Turning away from him to face Zelda, she said, "When can we get started? I need to know everything you know. Do you have the times and places these things happened, have you documented them?"

Zelda nodded. "As well as I could. Oh, Marcy, this will be such fun!" Her eyes widened, sparkling with excitement. "We could even have a séance up there. And I'll use my crystal ball. I know the perfect place. One time when I was exploring the house—"

"That's called trespassing."

She waved away Nick's grim interruption with an airy, "Nonsense, everyone does it. Anyway, I found a tiny room hidden behind some paneling. It will be perfect. We can do it there."

"The hell you will," Nick said.

Later that evening, Nick glanced up from his crossword puzzle to where Marcy was reading, curled up in the corner of the apricot couch across from him. "So you're a ghost buster."

"Hardly." Marcy placed a bookmark in the book she had borrowed from the small historical museum in town and closed it. The docent, thrilled that a professional writer was interested in their small town, had expressed her delight by pressing a wide assortment of books into Marcy's willing hands. "Not even close, as a matter of fact. I'm simply a writer, following the trail of an interesting story. Or, to be more accurate, following an idea with potential. They don't always work out, you know."

"What happens when they don't?"

Marcy shrugged. "I chalk up the time and energy spent to experience, keep the material and hope it will tie in with something else somewhere down the road."

"And if it doesn't?"

"Nothing's ever lost. I learned something and more than likely had fun doing it."

She put the book on the table beside her, waiting for the other shoe to fall. Nick had accompanied her into town earlier that day, stalking beside her as if he expected muggers to leap out of doorways or to materialize on the dusty wooden walkways behind them. They would have been utter fools if they had—assuming, of course, that there were any in the vicinity. The threat emanating from him was...daunting.

During the ride home she had pointed out at length how unnecessary his hovering was and hoped that her lecture would have some effect, that his self-imposed guard duty would end when they returned to the house.

It hadn't.

His lean body was toughened by his years on the force. At least she assumed that accounted for his particular brand of physical strength. It was a toughness that went right to his core, that affected his thoughts and emotions as well as his body. It gave him an edgy alertness, a wariness that the average ordinary citizen simply didn't have.

The trouble with Nick, Marcy reflected with a tinge of amusement, was that he'd been chasing bad guys too long.

He definitely needed to lighten up. He seemed to think that danger lurked behind every bush; unfortunately, this dry desert country abounded with bushes.

No, she reflected optimistically, what Nick Stoner needed was a new interest in life—something that would distract him from the dark side that he normally dealt with. And a friend. A pal—a *platonic* pal, she reminded herself—a buddy, someone who could make him laugh, someone who could help dispel the energy that sizzled through him like bacon frying in a pan.

With no more thought than that, other than the hope that she could divert the imminent and totally unnecessary lecture she saw coming, she said brightly, "You know, what I really need right now is a hardheaded realist. Someone who won't be distracted by Zelda's shenanigans and a spooky old house."

"And I suppose you want me to volunteer."

"Well," she said with a rueful smile, "you seem to be the only one around." She held up her hand to stop him before he could refuse. "I know what I said about going into a project unbiased, but the truth is, I really want to find a ghost."

Nick's lean face tightened. "I told you, I don't believe in ghosts."

"I know," she said with an approving nod, "that's exactly why I need you. As a member of the team," she added hastily, surprised and dismayed by the flare of sensual response in his dark eyes. The hunger, fierce as it was sudden, shouldn't have caught her off guard. She had seen glimpses of it all afternoon, a disquieting flicker of awareness and desire that she had refused to acknowledge. Was afraid to acknowledge, she admitted silently. Nick Stoner had all the earmarks of a loner, a tough, self-possessed man, and she didn't have the foggiest idea how to deal with his brand of sensuality.

Jolted, she sidestepped the issue and persevered. "I have a couple of editors who are very anxious to get their hands on a real, live ghost."

"A contradiction in terms if I ever heard one."

Marcy waved an impatient hand. "You know what I mean. And I'm just as bad. I want to find one. Too much to be as objective as I should be. What I need is a devil's advocate, and I don't know anyone better suited for the job." She waited, staring at his expressionless face. Finally, impatiently, she said, "Well? What do you think?"

"For starters," he said with a dangerous softness, "I think the whole situation is crazy. Your editors want a ghost and you want a ghost. Zelda, who is as loony as they come, knows there's a ghost, and she wants to see him in her crystal ball. You know what I want?"

"Uh, Nick . . ."

"I want you, Marcy O'Bannon," he said deliberately. "Now. Preferably without a stitch of clothes, in my bed. Hot and soft and clinging."

"*Nick,* for heaven's sake!"

"But I'll take you any way I can get you," he added. His voice was still soft, but he made no effort to conceal the hunger in his black eyes.

Marcy flinched at the restrained violence in his voice. She had underestimated him, she reflected moodily. Badly.

"That's not exactly what I meant," she began carefully.

"I know what you meant." Nick leaned back in the chair, challenging her with his inflexible gaze. "You thought you'd keep me so busy I wouldn't have time to think about you. About us."

He shook his head and smiled. It was not a comforting smile. "Let me tell you something, honey. There aren't enough distractions in the world to do that."

"This is impossible. *You're* impossible. How do you think I can work with a damned panther gliding around the place, looking like he's about to pounce."

"I never pounce," he said mildly. "You'll have plenty of warning."

"Damn it," she exploded, sitting straighter against the cushions and glaring at him. "Warning isn't what I want. I want a partner, someone to work with. Not a...a..."

"Lover?"

Marcy flushed at the blunt word. "How about just a friend?"

"No way." He shook his head slowly. "We'll never be just friends. Things went beyond that point the minute you walked in the door last night. You felt it then, you felt it this morning, and you're feeling it right now."

"Feeling what?"

His swift grin was as dangerous as his taut strength. "Chemistry. Tension. Call it whatever you want. We've got it. In spades. And someday—"

She held up her hand, interrupting him. "Whoa. Wait just a darn minute. Don't I have something to say about all this?" She took a calming breath and was infuriated to find it didn't help. "We both have our reasons for staying here," she began slowly, recalling Cristobel's letter and her plea. "I happen to think you're wrong about this, but I want your promise that you won't—"

He shook his head, stopping her cold. "Let me make this easy on both of us. I'll work with you on this crazy project. I'll be your devil's advocate. I'll save your neck if it needs saving. And while I'm doing it, I'll be trying my damnedest to get you in my bed.''

"Nick!"

"I'll make you one promise," he said levelly. "You'll be just as safe in my hands as you want to be."

Three

___

Nick sat on the patio, moodily watching Marcy's expressive face as she read the journal of one of Joshua Junction's pioneers. She wasn't just reading the material, he reflected, leaning back in the chair and propping his aching leg on a white wrought-iron table. She seemed to be soaking it through her pores, reacting both intellectually and emotionally as she read between the lines of the terse daily accounts.

He had learned something new about her in the two days since he'd agreed to work with her: Marcy did nothing in half measures. Whatever she did, she gave it her all. Whether she was simply walking, absorbing the scents and sounds of the land, or interviewing one of the senior residents in town, she did it with sensitivity and all the exuberance and anticipation of a kitten pouncing on a ball of string.

It was like being sidekick to a compassionate tornado.

She was stretched out on a lounge chair, wearing another one of her patented brief and clingy outfits. This one was light green. Sandals with paper-thin soles and two skimpy straps somehow clung to her slim bare feet. She might have been a princess, with nothing more urgent to do than sip daintily at her lemonade.

He grinned ruefully. Anyone who believed that was in for a big surprise. She was an energetic weapon aimed at an unsuspecting world, just resting between sorties. He almost felt as if he was just along for the ride. Almost. But since his instinct told him she was headed for trouble—and he had learned to trust that little voice—he was doing the only thing he could, sticking closer to her than a second skin.

Nothing had gone the way he had expected. But then how could it when he was dealing with a wild card like Marcy O'Bannon? Since she had involved him in this lunatic ghost hunt, he figured she owed him, so he was not only keeping a close watch on her, he was pushing, letting her know exactly how much he wanted her. And showing that he intended to have her.

And was she intimidated?

Hell, no.

She treated the matter as if it were a high-school outing, inviting him along for walks and interviews, acting as if she had a choice in the matter. And that was the problem—she didn't seem to realize that she didn't have a choice. That until this escapade was over, he was her shadow.

It wasn't only because he had promised Cristobel that he'd take care of things. That was a factor, but it wasn't the main one. In fact, he'd given little thought to his hostess since Marcy had flung open the front door and tried to kick a hole in his bad knee.

He wondered how she had survived in the real world for twenty-seven years. She obviously had mastered some practical skills along with her talent, but she seemed to live in a dream world, peopled by the characters in her stories. And if the clear, curious expression in her green eyes was any indication, she didn't have a clue about how she affected a man. Especially him. She'd probably be stunned to know that the memory of her sleek, little body moving under his when they'd wrestled on the floor had kept him awake every night since.

She was too damned trusting and didn't have the foggiest idea how dangerous the world really was. No, it was obvious that Marcy O'Bannon needed a keeper. It was just as obvious that he had a new job description. Aside from being a cop, he was now a guardian angel, a devil's advocate and a keeper.

And soon, a lover.

But it would take patience, because somewhere along the way Marcy had been burned, or at least singed, by a man. Whoever he was, he hadn't done too much damage, just enough to make her cautious. Enough to make her think it was safer to be a friend than a lover.

So he'd be patient. But fast.

As if she had heard her name called, Marcy looked up. "What?"

"You picking up Zelda's ESP?"

She grinned and set the journal aside. "You were making so much noise thinking, I'd have heard you in a thunderstorm."

Jolted, he stared at her, keeping his face expressionless. The last thing he needed was to have her turn into a mind reader. But she obviously didn't have a trace of psychic ability or she would have been at his throat by now. With that comforting thought, a trickle of relief eased the sudden tension in his shoulders. And if he was lucky, really lucky, it also meant that she wouldn't be so apt to get involved in Zelda's harebrained schemes.

Unwilling to push his luck, he headed for safer territory. "Last night I came across the scrapbook that Cristbel keeps for your articles."

"The one that weighs in at twenty pounds?" She gave him a look of mock sympathy. "She has a copy of everything I've ever written."

"I stayed up late last night, reading."

She waited expectantly. "And?" she finally prodded.

"You're good. Very good."

A smile, small and satisfied, curved her lips. "I know."

"And modest."

Marcy grinned. "Sorry, I couldn't resist it. Thank you, you've just said the words that every writer loves to hear. And for that, you get a reward. A nice, long walk to exercise your knee." She grabbed his hand and gave an optimistic tug, knowing full well that she couldn't budge his six feet of solid muscle if he didn't cooperate. "I want to see the old Mulroony place in the cold light of day."

"It's a wreck," he said flatly, obediently getting to his feet. "I went there once with Cristobel, and believe me, there's not much to see."

"I like wrecks. I want to see what there is about this one that stirs Zelda's imagination."

"All right, but you're not stepping foot inside the place," he warned her, locking the door and testing the dead bolt.

Marcy trotted down the stairs ahead of him. "Wouldn't dream of it," she assured him blithely.

"I mean it. The floors are probably rotted through."

"I'm sure they are."

He wrapped one hand around her upper arm, stopping her dead in her tracks. Gazing down into her startled eyes, he threatened softly, "I don't think you're taking me seriously, Marcy. You try to open a window or step on the porch, and I'll haul your cute butt back to the house so fast you won't know what hit you. When we get here, we'll have a long, serious talk about who's giving the orders and who's following them. Understand?"

Marcy blinked up at him in astonishment.

"I said, do you understand?"

"How could I not?" she snapped. "You've made yourself very clear."

"Good." Nick slid his hand down her arm, lacing his fingers through hers. He gently nudged her toward the curving two-lane road leading to the rutted dirt track that passed the Mulroony place and led to another similar road further back in the hills. "So tell me," he said in a casual voice, as if there had never been an interruption, "which story is your favorite?"

She considered both him and the question with a small, irritable frown, her green eyes narrowed. Annoyance flickered in her eyes, but her love of her craft apparently overcame her indignation. "That's a tough one," she finally said. "It's like asking a mother which child she likes best. It's never the article I'm working on, because that one is usually fraught with frustration of some sort. I'm normally pleased with the one I just finished and looking forward to the next one down the road. But I'm proud of all of them. If I'm not satisfied with one, I don't turn it in."

"As simple as that?"

She slanted a disbelieving look at him. "Don't kid yourself, it's not simple at all. At that point I'm dealing with looming deadlines and an editor's expectations. What we're talking is big-time stress."

"Why California folklore?"

"You mean, why do I specialize in it? Because it's fascinating. People from all over the world came to California, even before the gold rush. They were filled with dreams and most of them expected to work hard. Many were ambitious, some were corrupt. There are thousands of stories just waiting to be found. And told." She tried to tug her hand out of his but gave up when his fingers tightened, holding her palm firmly against his. Her eyes gleamed with unexpected humor when she added, "Besides, when I first started, there was a practical reason. I was here, I didn't have much money and I didn't have to travel far to do the research. It was cheap."

"So why change? You've got a good reputation in one field, why jump into another?"

"It fell in my lap like a ripe orange, and it's not really a different field. Only a different slant. One of my favorite magazines called and asked if I was interested in doing a series on California ghosts. It sounded intriguing and paid well. Very well. Coincidentally, that was the same time Cristobel called and told me about Zelda's Indian ghost." She grinned at him. "I was already interested. Cristobel's call clinched it. I wasn't about to question what the gods were handing me."

Nick stiffened. "Wait a minute. Series? Ghosts, as in plural?"

"Plural," Marcy affirmed cheerfully, her good humor restored by his dismay. Turning into the dirt road, which was little more than parallel ruts in the red soil, she said, "As in more than one. In this case, many more. San Diego is my next stop. They have some wonderful documented spooks. Zelda's ghost—"

"If there is one."

"—is new on the scene. Just think—" her laughing gaze met his—"I'll be breaking new ground here. I could be bringing a whole new concept in ghosts to the reading public. Maybe he's an environmentalist or—"

"Maybe he just likes to celebrate centennials," Nick finished dryly.

Pleased with herself, Marcy gazed around, studying the sloping ground. Chaparral, the dense thicket of hardy shrubs and dwarf trees that had adapted to the dry southern California summers, covered the hillside and ran down to the edge of the road. It was just as hot and dusty as it looked, with shades of green running the gamut from gray to olive drab. The only brilliant colors came from a few hardy wildflowers and the edible red fruit studding the clumps of prickly pear cacti.

"This is one steep hill," Marcy gasped as they neared the top. "Are you sure you should be doing this? Won't it bother your leg?"

"I'm fine."

Marcy's brows rose at his brusque reply. Cristobel would never forgive her if he damaged his knee following her around. She was considering how to pursue the matter when they stopped beside a huge boulder.

"Oh, look at that," she whispered, looking down on the majestic ruin. It stood alone at the near end of a small valley, a steep-roofed turret at each of the four corners towering over the rest of the two-story structure. It was a testament to neglect, missing shingles giving the roof a checkerboard effect. Many of the windows were either boarded up or cracked, adding to the ravaged effect of peeling paint and weathered wood.

"It's beautiful," Marcy said softly.

Nick slanted an amazed look at her. "Beautiful? It's falling apart."

"Now, yes. But imagine what it looked like when it was built. It was the pampered darling of a wealthy family. The windows were probably cleaned with vinegar water until they sparkled. The paint had a contrasting trim, and it must have looked like a fairy-tale house."

She tightened her grasp on his hand and tugged him forward, her eyes gleaming with enthusiasm. "Come on, I want to peek through the windows. Can you imagine what the inside looks like? It probably has real wood paneling and chests. And the kitchen. Oh, Nick, the kitchen must be gorgeous, with a built-in pantry and cupboards."

As they picked their way down through the scrubby growth, Marcy kept up a running commentary. "They should have planted pine trees on the hill behind them and maples in the front yard, with the leaves turning scarlet and gold in the fall. And a huge circle of grass running around the house like a bright green skirt."

He looked down at her with a grin. "You really are a romantic, aren't you?"

"Don't ever doubt it." Noting the care he took to step on level ground, she gave him a quick frown and said, "Nick, are you really all right? We shouldn't be climbing like this. You could slide on these pebbles and—"

"I'm fine," he said shortly.

Marcy shot him a look of utter exasperation. "Will you quit acting like you have to be Superman all the time? I'm just . . . concerned."

Nick sighed and gave her hand a quick squeeze. "Sorry. I didn't mean to . . ."

"Bite my head off?"

He gave her a long look. "Yeah. I know what I'm doing. As long as I balance my weight and watch where I'm going, everything's fine. Come on, let's get down there."

As they approached the house, Marcy stopped and looked around with a puzzled glance. "I thought Zelda said the town had been built over the Indian village. The town's back that way a few miles." She pointed back in the direction they had walked.

"Fire," Nick said absently, giving the house an assessing glance. "Cristobel said that everything but this place burned down about ninety years ago. When the city fathers rebuilt, they decided to move to where they are now. Some local hotshot thought the train was coming through that way. Come on, let's go around this way."

As they circled the house, Marcy kept throwing wistful glances at it. "Nick, couldn't we just—"

"No." He pointed to the back porch. "See that? The boards that aren't loose are riddled with termites. The place looks like a stiff wind would blow it over."

"How about just peeking in the windows?"

"They're too high." He cast a critical glance at the nearest one. "Even if we could reach them, we couldn't see anything. They're cruddy."

Marcy gave a disgruntled sigh. "Never go ghost hunting with a practical man," she grumbled.

"You're the one who invited him along," he reminded her unsympathetically.

"So I did. It wasn't one of my better ideas. Uh...Nick?"

"Hmm?"

She hesitated then plunged ahead. "I'd like to be alone for a while, so I can...let my imagination run loose. I need to get the feel of the place."

She eyed his skeptical expression and grinned. "No, I promise, I won't try to break in. I just want to sit quietly and soak up the atmosphere." She considered the hard planes of his face for another long moment, then said brightly, "While I'm doing that, maybe you can snoop around and find some muggers."

Nick ignored her feeble attempt at humor. Instead, he inspected every square inch of the yard as if he expected a band of terrorists to storm them.

"Ten minutes." The reluctant words were somewhere between a promise and a threat.

"Fifteen."

"Twelve and a half." When she started to protest, he said evenly, "It's that or nothing."

"Twelve and a half," she agreed hastily. Waving her hand in a shooing gesture, she said, "Go."

He went, but not without one last long look. "You promised," he reminded her, waiting for her nod. When he rounded the corner, he glanced at his watch.

Exactly twelve and a half minutes later he came back to find Marcy perched on a large, flat rock with her legs crossed tailor fashion. Her eyes were closed and the backs of her hands rested lightly on her knees. His brows rose as he noted the ease with which she remained on her precarious roost. So meditation was a comfortable part of her life. Another facet. But if serenity was her goal, he reflected, it apparently wasn't working. A small frown drew her brows together.

When Marcy opened her eyes, her green eyes were soft and inviting. She blinked, her lingering gaze absorbing his sudden tension, the hard cast to his face. Color flooded her cheeks and stunned awareness fleetingly darkened her eyes, increasing the depth of invitation. Then, with an effort he couldn't help but admire, she blinked and smiled at him. It was not an alluring, inviting smile, he noted absently, but a valiant attempt to ignore the stab of sensuality and get on with the business at hand.

That over with, she unfolded her legs with unconscious grace and scooted forward. Nick wrapped his hands around her small waist and lifted. He swung her down so swiftly, so easily, she lost her footing and stumbled against him. When she grabbed for his shoulders, his arms closed around her, pulling her close, holding her against him.

Forever.

From shoulders to knees, molding her softness to his hard body.

Sharing searing heat, blatant arousal and a jolting charge of electricity.

"No!" Her protest was breathless and a bit flustered, but Marcy finally tugged free and stepped back, severing the connection.

Nick followed, stopping when she shook her head. "Why not?"

"Because."

"That's one hell of a nonanswer."

"All right then, because I've known you for exactly three days and it's too soon for... this." She waved an agitated hand between them, indicating what *this* meant. "Good grief, Nick, the only thing we have in common is the commitment we have to our jobs."

"And this," he said evenly, repeating the word and letting it fall in the silence between them. "I want you, Marcy. In every way that a man can want a woman." He touched a fiery strand of her hair, his lean fingers gentle against the rapid pulse in her throat. "And what's scaring the hell out of you is that you want me just as bad. You can't walk away from it any more than I can."

Opting to do just that, Marcy turned on her heel and started back to the house, moving briskly. "Wrong, Nick."

She took a shaky breath. "In a couple of weeks you'll be back on the job, terrorizing bad guys, and I'll be off chasing more ghosts."

"And in the meantime, we pretend that we're two friends who just happen to be staying in the same house?"

She ignored the sarcasm, pouncing on the suggestion as if it were the solution to world peace. "Exactly." Her smile was relieved.

"You think we can?"

"Of course we can," she said stoutly.

His dark eyes asked who she was kidding. "At times, your optimism is mind-boggling."

The trip back was silent. Nick waved Marcy ahead of him when they climbed the hill. He wanted to be behind her if she slipped, even if the sway of her sweet tush made him think of hauling her back into his arms and really giving her something to worry about. The position also had the advantage of keeping her anxious green eyes off him every time he took a step.

They were almost back at the house before Marcy hesitated, looking over her shoulder at him. Nick gave a silent groan. He knew what that particular blend of bravado and determination meant: Marcy was simply going to ignore what had just happened between them. She was back to being his buddy, his partner in the big ghost chase.

"So," she said with forced cheerfulness, "I forgot to ask if you found any bad guys while you were snooping around."

"Not this time." She really was going to try it! He gave her a rueful smile and watched the confidence pour back into her eyes. "But there's always hope."

"Ever the cop," she murmured, opening the screen door.

"Right. The only interesting thing I saw was some tire tracks. Off roaders by the looks of them. But it's probably just some kids going out there to knock off some beer. What about you?"

Marcy stiffened. "What *about* me?"

Nick shrugged. "I just wondered if you saw anything while I was gone."

Waiting just a fraction too long, Marcy said quickly, "No. Nothing."

Nick's eyes narrowed. He watched as color seeped into her cheeks. "Marcy."

At the quiet warning, she said crossly, "For heaven's sake, Nick, we were out there all by ourselves. What was there to see?"

Midnight.

The witching hour.

And Nick had finally gone to bed.

Marcy zipped the dark jeans and pulled on a navy blue sweatshirt over her blouse. The days might be hotter than blazes in this semidesert country, but southern Californians were usually blessed with cool nights. She had deliberately selected the clothes for her expedition with a dual purpose in mind—warmth and concealment.

She slid a black, loosely knit cap on her head, tucking her long hair beneath the brim. Looking into the mirror for the first time, she wrinkled her nose. All she lacked was some of the black gunk smeared on her face that soldiers used for camouflage and she'd be mistaken for a gung-ho survivalist. But she wouldn't need the stuff for a ghost, and with any luck at all Nick wouldn't set his clock for sentry duty.

Marcy opened the door and crept down the hall, grateful that Nick was sleeping on the other side of the house.

Even so, her palms were damp and her breath was trapped deep in her lungs. She had a sneaking suspicion that he was right; she *was* a lousy burglar. And it wasn't going to be any easier getting out than it had been getting in—especially with the fancy new locks that he'd installed on all the doors and windows.

Fully expecting the scream of an alarm, she reached out a shaky hand to flick open the lock and tug at the window. When it slid up, smoothly and silently, she climbed through, dangled from the sill for a moment then dropped quietly to the ground, her running shoes muffling the sound. Jogging down the curving road with a triumphant grin, she speculated optimistically about an article on cat burglars. People were fascinated with the subject, lured by the element of risk, and what the heck, when researching, a little personal experience never hurt.

Nick was going to have her head if he found out about this little escapade. The memory of his taut face when he'd exacted her promise not to enter the Mulroony house brushed through her mind. But that promise had been for then, she reminded herself virtuously. Not for now. Besides, she didn't intend to go in. She didn't even plan to get very close. All she wanted was a few minutes alone, to absorb the ambience.

Marcy grinned in the darkness, thinking how Nick the pragmatic cop would have a field day with that word. She assumed he didn't concern himself about foolish things like ambience; he gathered clues, slapped on handcuffs and wrote reports. At least, that's what cops in the movies did. Oh, well, if she was lucky, she wouldn't be in a position to learn how he felt about such things as vibes and atmosphere.

Actually, it didn't matter how he felt about them. But they were an important element of her work—as vital as the information itself. Facts touched the readers' intellect, but it was the emotional impact that hooked them. And she was good at hooking them, she assured herself as she followed the rutted tracks. Damned good. But first she had to care, she had to find an element that touched her emotions.

Which brought her full circle. That's why she was here, wandering down a deserted road under a star-studded sky. She had to find out if the uneasy feeling she'd had earlier that day was related to the old house or if it was simply a reaction to Nick's edgy mood.

The speculation brought Zelda and her blasted crystal ball to mind. The older woman might have some psychic ability, but Marcy knew with absolute certainty that she, Marcy O'Bannon, did not. Yes, she had empathy and a vivid imagination, two elements that enabled her to "see" her subjects in living color. And over the years she had learned to trust her instincts. She also had hunches. But that was it. No spooky messages from Zelda's busy spirit world. Nothing. *Nada.*

So what was the explanation for the eerie episode this afternoon? Marcy shivered despite her warm clothes.

She topped the crest of the hill and looked down at the huge, old house. In the light of day it had been dispirited, a worn shadow of its former proud beauty. At night, all the potential was there. It seemed possible that the lights could suddenly blaze through the windows to reveal people dressed in clothes that were in vogue a century ago. Music could fill the air, encouraging couples to dance or to gather around the piano and blend their voices in song. The fragrance of jasmine could drift through the windows, inviting lovers to seek privacy in a rose-covered bower.

Easing down on a large, flat rock that still held a remnant of the day's heat, she gazed at the house. Yes, if one were fanciful enough, anything was possible. Well, God only knew that she was *that,* all right. That particular quality went with her territory.

But she wasn't crazy, and what had happened that afternoon definitely fell in that category. She stared down at the house, willing it to reveal its secrets.

Had someone really called for help? Had another almost inaudible voice, urgent and cracked, cried out for her to run?

Marcy couldn't swear that she had heard anything; in fact, if asked, she would have to admit that she probably hadn't. It had been more like an intrusive thought. And if that were the case, she wondered wryly, where had it come from? The past—over a hundred years ago? Or her overactive imagination?

She had been mulling over those questions when Nick had returned, and one glance at his hard face settled the issue: she wasn't going to open that particular can of worms with him. She was in no mood for a lecture on hysteria and psychic instability.

She crossed her legs beneath her, took a deep breath and tried to clear her mind, to concentrate on the house.

Or nothing.

Or anything except Nick.

The problem, she reflected, squirming restlessly on the hard surface, was that the voices—or imagined voices—had shaken her, setting her up for what followed. And Nick the thug—the man who vowed he didn't pounce—sensing an opening, had pounced.

Thirty minutes later, Marcy gave up in disgust. She had a feeling that she could sit there until dawn and still not clear her mind. At that point, she wasn't even certain what she had hoped to accomplish by coming to the house.

At least, she reflected with relief, she hadn't heard that awful voice again.

Of course, it was possible that she was too far away, but she doubted it. She swung her legs over the edge of the rock, admitting that there were all sorts of possibilities, the most reasonable being that her imagination had been working overtime earlier that afternoon. Nothing had really happened. Nothing at all. There were no voices. No cries for help. No warnings.

Fine. So be it.

She slid to her feet and swiped at the back of her jeans, firmly putting the whole matter out of her mind. Now all she had to worry about was finding a ghost, dealing with a loony psychic and . . . Nick.

Marcy shivered and started up the hill. Nick. It had occurred to her more than once in the last few days that she didn't know much about him except that he had a penchant for rescuing stray women.

But—she stopped so abruptly she teetered precariously and almost slid back down—that wasn't true. She knew he was a man who dealt with darkness and violence on a daily basis. He had a protective streak a mile wide and a lean strength that was both intimidating and intriguing. He was a renegade, a modern-day pirate. And with just a fleeting touch of his hand, he turned her body to fire. He had a killer smile, and though he hadn't even kissed her, he had already sensitized her to his touch.

Marcy reached the crest of the hill at the same time she reached a decision. She was absolutely not going to worry about Nick Stoner. She had other priorities. She had to find a ghost. She had to write an article. She had to... Marcy glanced at her watch, groaned softly and started trotting down the badly paved road.

She had to get back through that blasted window before Nick woke up and found her gone.

Four

"**D**amn!"

Ten minutes later Marcy stood beneath the open window, swearing softly. It was too high. Impossibly high. At least ten inches above her groping fingertips.

Staring up in disgust at the open window, she wondered why she hadn't recognized that small detail and done something about it before she'd jumped. Of course, any of her stolid, unimaginative male relatives would have been happy to inform her why. It was because she was too impulsive, too impetuous. Because, except for her writing schedule, she didn't know the meaning of the phrase "plan ahead."

Well, now what? She couldn't get back inside without the aid of a ladder, which of course Nick had tidily locked up in the garage. Or a step stool which was inconveniently inside the house in the pantry. Or a trash can which Mr. Neat had efficiently secured in a metal storage bin. One comprehensive glance around was enough to assure her that there wasn't anything in the yard large enough to aid and abet a burglar, especially a bungling one.

As she gloomily considered various alternatives, ranging from pogo sticks to trampolines, the moon broke through a drift of low clouds, illuminating the area as thoroughly as a spotlight on a darkened stage. Right on cue, a hard male voice silkily inquired, "Got a problem?"

"Nick!" She jumped back and stared at the opening above her. "You scared the life out of me. What on earth are you doing up at this time of night?"

After a charged silence, he said mildly, "Good question. I was about to ask you the same thing." He stuck his head out of the window, resting his elbows on the sill. "Hold up your hands."

A sense of déjà vu enveloped her as she looked up at him. At that angle he appeared naked and lethal, just as he had seemed that first night. The moonlight frosting his dark hair etched implacable shadows on his face and made him appear even more intimidating than he was.

"Uh, why don't you just open the front door?" Marcy asked reasonably.

"For an intrepid cat burglar like you?" he scoffed. "Too tame." He extended his arms. "Come on, it's a piece of cake."

It wasn't getting up that bothered her, Marcy mused, looking at his large hands. She knew he wouldn't drop her. He had the strength to lift her without her help if he had to. It was what was going to happen after she climbed through the window that worried her.

"Marcy," he snapped. "Do it. Now."

She reached up, and his large hands closed around her wrists. After that, it was surprisingly simple. With a minimum of fuss, he hoisted her up and she clambered through the window. As soon as her feet touched the floor, she broke away, moving across the room.

"Don't even think about it," he warned in a level voice. "You're not going anywhere until we talk." Nick followed her, turning on a lamp when she came to a stop by a cushioned sofa.

"That was a slick maneuver," she told him brightly, busily swatting at the knees of her jeans. He was, she noted with relief, not naked. He was wearing his jeans. "We ought to consider forming a team."

"I thought we had."

Marcy stilled as he extended his hand and pulled the knit cap off her head. Something heated and dangerous flickered in his eyes as he watched her hair tumble down around her shoulders.

"You're angry," she hazarded, backing up a step and giving him a conciliatory smile.

"Damn straight, lady." He tossed the cap aside, his dark gaze never leaving her face. Ignoring her smile, he said, "I passed angry when I found you gone. Right now, I'm mad as hell. Just what do you think you were doing out there?"

"I didn't go in the house." The words came out in a rush and she briefly closed her eyes, her apologetic tone annoying her immensely.

He repeated the words slowly, then once again, spacing them with deliberate emphasis. "You didn't go in the house? Damn it, Marcy, are you telling me you went out to the Mulroony place? Alone?"

"Of course I did." Her voice was muffled as she pulled the sweatshirt over her head. Tossing it on the arm of the couch, she said, "Where else would I go? This isn't exactly a thriving metropolis, you know."

"I thought you were at Zelda's. Of course," he said in a carefully neutral tone, "I wondered why you found it necessary to go through a window, but I thought—"

"Nick—"

"—that you might have some charming eccentricity about using doors after midnight."

"—I can explain."

"You promised, Marcy." His anger was controlled but evident in the three bitten off words.

Her gaze lifted to the ceiling in exasperation. "I knew you were going to say that. I just *knew* it."

"Well, damn it, you did."

"Don't swear at me." She scowled at him. "Besides, that was this afternoon."

"So what are you saying, promises you make before dinner don't count?"

"Listen to me, Nick Stoner." She spaced her words with the same deliberation, the same emphasis. "I made that promise this afternoon *for* this afternoon. I promised you that I wouldn't go in the house for the twelve and a half minutes that you were gone. I didn't. I kept my promise. Once you were back, the slate was clean."

His fingers raked through his hair, and he stared down at her as if she were some rare, alien form. "Clean?"

She nodded. "Clean. I lived up to my promise."

With a heavy hand on her shoulder, Nick urged her down onto the sofa. "We have to talk," he told her grimly, dropping beside her.

"Nick, it's after one. Can't we have this discussion in the morning?"

"Not if I'm going to get any sleep the rest of the night."

"Okay." She sighed a bit more dramatically than the situation warranted, but she had a nasty feeling that she knew where he was heading. Nick intended to wring a blanket guarantee out of her, an all-purpose warranty that would ensure his peace of mind for the next few weeks. She slanted a quick look at him and just as quickly turned away. Fully clothed, Nick was... distracting. Half naked he was a menace—especially to a woman who was dealing with the issue of self-preservation, one who was doing her level best to maintain a safe distance.

Marcy shifted restlessly, sternly lecturing herself. She could handle this. She was an O'Bannon, right? Right. She had her priorities straight, right? Right!

Then why did she want to just sit and drink in the sight of him? Why did she need to know if his hard mouth would soften when he kissed her, if it was as seductive as it looked? Why did she want to run her fingertips over his tan skin, tracing his shoulders and testing the texture of the crisp dark hair that fanned over his chest and formed a narrow line down his belly? Why did she want to press her lips to a thin arc of a scar below his left nipple?

Because she was crazy, right? Right.

And because she was crazy—but not that crazy—she would look, and wonder a little, but not touch. She would try to keep him off balance until she finished this job, then both she and her determined bodyguard would go their respective ways. Until then...

She turned to him with wide eyes. "I almost forgot, Zelda asked when we're going to get together with her and Gray Feather for a séance."

"When hell freezes over." His hand cupped her thigh, tugging gently until she was pressing against him. Even through the fabric of her jeans she could feel the heat of him. "But that's not what I want to talk about."

"I think we're missing something," she said thoughtfully. "It seems to me that if we're going to find this ghost, we have to try everything we can. I know Zelda's gone off the deep end and at times sounds a little . . . strange—"

"A *little?*"

"—but we don't have a heck of a lot to work with. I'm willing," she said persuasively. "Don't you want to learn more about it? Who knows—you might find it handy in your job someday."

Nick leaned forward, the weight of his chest trapping her gently against the back of the sofa, his dark eyes holding her gaze with the same implacable force. "Honey, I assure you, I would *never* use that stuff in my job. What I want to know has nothing to do with a séance, and I've just decided that I can't wait another second to find out."

His lips muffled her startled protest, brushed hers gently, then returned, testing, savoring. "You taste just the way I thought you would," he muttered. "Damp and warm with a sweet fire." His fingers brushed her ear, tracing the delicate curve, lingering on the velvety softness of her cheek, touched her shoulder and then moved hungrily to the gentle curve of her breast. "And you feel even better. Soft and hot and inviting."

Marcy shivered when his thumb grazed her nipple, stroked it to a taut bead of exquisite sensitivity. His lips— yes, she thought hazily, they did soften, were definitely seductive—drank in her gasp, and even she recognized the hungry femininity of her soft cry.

"I've wanted you for a lifetime," he muttered, slowly freeing her mouth to explore the tender curve of her shoulder. "Marcy."

"Mmmm?"

"Touch me. Put your hands on me."

Her fingers rested tentatively on his shoulders before moving slowly down his chest. "Here?"

He groaned his approval. "For starters. I need to feel you. Everywhere." He pulled her closer and her arms slid around him, one hand working down his bare back to trace the straight line of his spine. He groaned again. "Ah, Marcy. Sweetheart, keep me from going out of my mind. Let me take care of you."

"Mmmm." She shivered and arched her neck, inviting his touch, needing it.

"Tell me that you will."

"Oh, Nick." His words didn't register. She would listen later, she promised herself hazily. Later, when he wasn't turning her to fire. Her sigh was half demand, half plea, made as she twined her arms around his neck and nestled closer.

"Promise me, honey."

"What?" she whispered huskily, dazed by his sensual assault.

His strong hands cradled the back of her head, thumbs moving along the line of her jaw until her dazed eyes met his gaze. "What?" she repeated softly, touching his cheek with gentle, questing fingertips.

"Promise me you won't go anywhere without me, that you'll let me take care of you."

Marcy stilled, finally hearing his words, finally heeding the inner warning she had been ignoring. Then she blinked, reluctantly acknowledging that the seduction was over. Oh, the words were tender enough, she assured herself. They were words designed to melt any woman's resistance. But this woman had heard them often enough to know that Nick the cop was back on duty, using whatever means he had at his disposal to get what he wanted.

Even seduction.

She closed her eyes and took a quick sustaining breath before leaning back to look up at him. If she hadn't been prepared, the determination in his black eyes would have been as shocking as a splash of icy water, bringing her back to earth with a nasty jolt.

"What did you say?" she asked quietly.

There was no need to ask. He had touched her with a lover's touch, played her like a damned piano to get what he wanted. He knew exactly what he was doing and precisely what he was saying.

"I said—"

"Never mind." She braced her fingers on his chest and pressed. "I heard you. Finally. Let me go, Nick."

"Marcy—"

"I want you to take your hands off of me. Now!" She pushed harder and waited.

"Sweetheart—"

"*Now,* Nick."

Gazing down at her frozen face, Nick swore and released her. When she jumped to her feet and paced across the room, he followed, saying, "I was simply trying to—"

Marcy swung around, glaring at him. "To what, Nick? Manipulate me? Make me agree to anything?" The fact that he had come dangerously close to doing exactly that merely served to escalate her fury. "Well, you had the wrong plan and the wrong woman. If you're into games like that, you're going to have to find another playmate."

"Damn it, Marcy, listen to me." He put a hand on her shoulder to stop her agitated pacing. "I wasn't playing games, I was trying to save your stubborn neck!"

"From what?" She stopped long enough to shrug off his hand, then headed back to the window. "Who are you saving me from, Nick? A ghost that you don't believe in? From Zelda? Gray Feather? There's no one else around here but us chickens, Nick."

"That we know of," he said quietly.

She spun around, her green eyes blazing. "Don't you think that sounds just a wee bit paranoid?" She didn't wait for an answer. "Well, I do. Either that or you're so used to being in control, you simply need to have everything run according to your plans."

Marcy took another deep breath and cast an oblique glance at Nick. He hadn't moved a muscle. He was like any other predator, she thought disgustedly, with the ability to remain absolutely still, watching and waiting until his prey wore itself out. In this case, she reminded herself, she was the prey, and if she displayed any weakness, he would just swoop down and take over.

"It's not going to work that way," she told him quietly. "Not this time. I'm going to do my job and I'm going to do it the way I always do, following whatever leads I find, accepting whatever help is offered. I'm not going to make any promises to you. None."

"Damn it, Marcy, I just want to take care of you. Is that so terrible? All I'm asking is a little cooperation from you."

Marcy shoved back her hair with a weary gesture. "I think you've been a cop for too long, Nick. You expect trouble and danger everywhere you look. Well, I'm not going to live under that kind of a dark shadow. I enjoy my work and the kind of life I lead, and I don't intend to change the way I do things."

"And what if something does happen?" Nick didn't try to hide his irritation.

"Like what?" she challenged. "If I actually do find a ghost? I doubt if I'll be in any physical danger." Of course she might be scared out of her wits, Marcy admitted silently. The thought of encountering one of the risen dead in a spooky mansion was a hair-raising thought. "From what I've heard, he seems more inclined to flash lights and make noise than threaten people," she added, hoping she sounded braver than she felt. "Besides, even if he turned out to be a homicidal maniac, bullets wouldn't help."

"I'd probably end up feeling sorry for the poor sucker," Nick said grimly. "I'm feeling a little homicidal myself, right now. All I'm trying to say is—"

"That you feel perfectly justified making love to a woman, even if you have an ulterior motive." Marcy's cool words stopped Nick in his tracks. "Well, I disagree. I told you the first night how I felt about my privacy. I feel even more strongly about this issue." That was putting it mildly. If a man was hell-bent on seducing her, it had damn well better be because he couldn't wait to get her in bed, not because he wanted to win an argument.

A sudden yawn startled her, reminding her that she had had a long and harrowing day. "Good night," she said quietly, picking up her cap and heading for the door. "I'm turning in. It's long past my bedtime." She turned back to face him, her hand resting on the knob. "I don't know what you want to do about the next couple of weeks."

Nick had his supercop expression on; it didn't give away a thing. Neither did his voice. "Don't start mincing words now, Marcy. What are you trying to tell me?"

She didn't know. She was mad enough to toss him out the door and hope he landed on his bum knee, but Cristobel's debt and her plea kept Marcy quiet. There was another consideration, she admitted with silent honesty. If she was going to encounter a ghost, Nick, with his outspoken skepticism and considerable strength, was far superior as a backup to Zelda and her crystal ball.

And there was yet another reason, she reflected, looking at his proud and furious face. One that she was too angry right now to even consider.

"Tell you?" she finally said. "Only this. As long as you remember what I said earlier, you don't have to leave on my account."

The next morning Marcy sat in Zelda's kitchen, her pen poised over a brand-new spiral-bound pad.

It was her one concession to the organizational mania that plagued writers of all genres and the answer to the inevitable dilemma: how to retrieve information at a later date, or more simply how to keep pertinent data at one's fingertips. Marcy had known up front that maintaining impeccable files was not high on her list of priorities, so she had opted for stark simplicity—a new notebook for each article. Both a copy of the article and the pad were ultimately numbered, crammed into a folder, along with any miscellaneous data, and dropped into a filing cabinet. A separate cross-reference file itemizing the number and article title completed the process.

Normally the system worked flawlessly. But this morning, she admitted with silent disgust, nothing was working. The notebook was in the same pristine state it had been in when she'd grabbed it and hustled out of the house before Nick had gotten up. She supposed it could be because she hadn't gotten much sleep—actually none at all, if the truth be known. Then again, it might be because Zelda was, to put it politely, a true original. Putting it bluntly, she was a fruitcake. Nothing she said made a whit of sense.

There was a third reason, one that made her a bit tense— if not downright edgy. Nick hadn't said a thing in his defense the night before and he wasn't a man to remain silent, unless for some obscure reason it suited him to do so. She had learned to her dismay that he could be painfully blunt on occasion. So she was waiting for the other shoe to fall, a situation that was becoming a familiar one around him, she reflected, shifting restlessly on the kitchen chair. Actually, she was waiting for him to barge through the back door and haul her someplace where they would finish the argument she had walked away from.

If that happened, it was definitely going to be a case of good news, bad news. Good, because she hated the tension resulting from unresolved issues, in this particular case she hated walking around on eggshells and sneaking out to avoid confronting Nick. Bad, because she had lost the fine edge of adrenaline supplied by her rage the night before. Her family had often compared her temper to a Fourth of July rocket—flash and fury and a lot of fizzle.

She simply couldn't carry a grudge. The fact was both a blessing and a curse. She would never end up with ulcers, but it left her at a distinct disadvantage in confrontations once her anger had cooled. So if he did come, she was not in a favorable position, especially when dealing with a man who was obviously accustomed to winning.

"Let's try it again, Zelda," she said patiently. "So far, we've established that there are no witnesses. No one has made a complaint, and the police aren't investigating the matter. Am I right so far?"

"Right." Zelda bobbed her head, sending her tight curls into a frenzy of activity.

"Have you called the police?"

"Of course not!"

"Why not?"

"Because the officials of our world neither understand nor deal effectively with the spirit world." She paused and upended a paper sack over two cereal bowls, pouring a mound of organic grains into each dish. "Besides," she added in a more practical voice, "if I had done that, we would've had reporters up here tramping all over the place and driving us crazy. Here, have some of this." She slid a bowl in front of Marcy. "Gray Feather recommends it. It clears the channels."

"Whose channels?"

Zelda shrugged and plunked a carton of milk on the table. "Eat."

"I wouldn't, if I were you," Nick said calmly.

Marcy spun around in her seat, her eyes rounded with surprise. He was leaning in the doorway leading to the living room, a white paper sack dangling from one hand. Trust him to come in behind her, making no more noise than a cat, she thought disgustedly. More of his supercop training, no doubt.

"Put away the birdseed, Zelda." Nick pushed away from the door and ambled over to the table, waggling the white sack. "I brought goodies."

Staring fixedly at the dark hair dusting the back of his hands, Marcy said, "We were just about to—uh, clear some channels."

"Trust me on this one," Nick said easily, snagging the leg of one chair with his foot and pulling it out. "Don't do it. Whatever Gray Feather said about the stuff, he lied."

She wasn't quite sure how he did it, but within seconds he had them organized. Marcy selected mugs and poured the coffee, while Zelda whipped up some scrambled eggs and Nick produced muffins from the bag with all the flair of a magician pulling a rabbit from a hat. The conversation inevitably returned to the ghost.

"There's something I still don't understand," Marcy said, breaking off a bit of muffin and popping it in her mouth.

Nick grinned. "Just one?"

"For now." Her lips curving in a reluctant smile, she looked at the woman sitting across from her. "If no one has complained, and if neither the police nor the media know anything about it, who does know about this famous ghost?''

Zelda blinked, her astonishment at the question apparent to both of them. "I know. And Cristobel—I told her as soon as I figured it out. And now the two of you. And, of course, Gray Feather."

"So it's just the four of us."

"Five," Zelda amended.

Nick gave Marcy a bland smile. "Your editors will be overjoyed. An undocumented ghost, and you'll be first with the big news."

Marcy frowned. "Zelda, there are holes in this thing big enough for an elephant to walk through. What started it? Why are you so convinced we've got a ghost? And don't, for God's sake, tell me it's because Gray Feather said so!"

"He didn't tell me. Not exactly. He doesn't talk the way you and I talk. We communicate in symbols. Of course, I'm new at it and I don't always—"

"The ghost," Nick said firmly.

Zelda sighed and shot him a look of mild reproof. "It all began about six months ago, on my evening walks. The road out to the Mulroony place makes a good track. It's a little over two miles, round trip."

Nick leaned back, snagged the coffeepot and refilled their cups. "I've never seen you go out in the evening."

"*Late* evening, usually after eleven or twelve. It's nice then, quiet. A perfect time to meditate as I walk."

"Oh, God," he groaned. "Another midnight roamer."

"I saw the lights on several occasions," she said definitely. "Not every night, you understand. They came at intervals, somewhere between one and two weeks."

Marcy put down her muffin and stared at the older woman. "You saw lights at the house? Isn't the electricity cut off?"

Zelda shook her head. "I was on the other side of the hill when I saw them. I don't think they came from the house. It was as if that section of the valley was washed in light, and it was visible over the crest of the hill, like an aura."

"What about the dogs?" Marcy picked up her pen, added a few words and flipped to a clean page.

"I heard people talking at the store in town. There were nights when all the dogs in the area would raise cain. Eventually, I started putting things together and realized that those occasions always coincided with the lights."

"Did you ever go over the hill when you saw the lights?"

"Of *course!*" Zelda gave her an affronted look. "But they only lasted for a second, almost like a flash of lightning. When I looked down, the place seemed normal— pitch-black and abandoned. I even started taking my binoculars, but I never saw a living thing. Of course," she added in a practical voice, "I never saw a dead thing, either."

"And the cries? Who heard them?"

For the first time, Zelda hesitated. "I did. On three occasions," she said slowly, a troubled look in her brown eyes. "They were—" she shivered and laced her fingers around her cup "—quite awful. Eldritch. Like witch's laughter in a bad Hollywood film."

Marcy dropped her pen and stared.

"Doesn't sound like a stoic Indian to me," Nick said laconically.

Giving a reluctant nod, Marcy agreed. "Nick's right. Where's the connection? What makes you think the ghost—if there is a ghost—is Indian?"

Zelda gave her a look a teacher might give a slow student. "Because of the feathers."

Nick swore, and Marcy's gaze rose to the ceiling. "What feathers?" she asked through clenched teeth.

"The ones I'd find in the Mulroony yard the day after I'd see the lights. Six times, six feathers." She beamed at them and gave Marcy a reassuring pat on the hand. "Gray Feather is convinced that they're a message from an Indian who's made his transition. I believe him."

Marcy closed her notebook with a snap. "I think I'm on overload," she said feebly.

After that, the conversation drifted from one topic to another, and it wasn't until they were walking back to Cristobel's house that Nick said, "Well, what do you think? Do you buy the ghost theory?"

Lifting a shoulder in a small shrug, she waited while he held the door for her. As she walked inside, she shook her head. "I don't know. The whole thing keeps getting weirder and weirder. What do you think?"

Nick put his hands on her shoulder and brought her to a halt. "I think I want to talk about last night. No, hold still. This time, you're not leaving until I've said my piece." His temper was under control, but remnants of it gleamed in his dark eyes. Temper and another emotion she had come to recognize quite easily—frustrated passion.

"I wasn't trying to manipulate you last night," he said grimly. "I was just trying to clear up some old business before we became lovers."

Five

The weatherman had promised a storm, the good, old-fashioned electrical type. Marcy grinned as she stepped into her dark jeans. It couldn't have come at a better time. Rain in southern California was always an event, and the promise of a slam-bang gully washer generated almost as much excitement as winning the lottery. It was also a good distraction, and the tumultuous wind would cover any noise she might make getting in and out of the house.

Everyone was talking about the weather—newscasters, reporters, the people in town, Zelda. For all Marcy knew, even Gray Feather had made a few pertinent comments about it, in symbols of course.

Marcy zipped her jeans and ambled over to her bedroom window, watching for the occasional show of lightning that pricked the threatening sky. A restless surge of energy licked through her veins, matching the eddying wind ruffling the long leaves of the eucalyptus trees and moaning as it buffeted the stucco house.

Yep, she decided, returning to her earlier train of thought, the storm was undoubtedly a good topic of conversation, and considering the number of subjects that had become sensitive issues—their status as "lovers," ghosts, psychics and the Mulroony place—she had taken full advantage of it.

Maybe it was true that every cloud came down the pike with a silver lining, Marcy thought, pulling her sweatshirt and running shoes out of the closet. Because once the incipient rain had been thoroughly assessed and discussed, the atmosphere had lightened enough for her to grill Nick. Of course she had been more adroit than that, she recalled with a satisfied grin. Over the past few years she had probably conducted enough interviews to be listed in Guinness, and the experience had taught her to pry open the tightest of clams. And to manage it so gently they thought they were doing it themselves.

So Nick had talked. About his family—parents, two married sisters and assorted nieces and nephews, all living in the San Diego area. And about his job. He'd told stories of his daily routine, of chases, arrests and the bad guys who got away. Not too many of those, he assured her. He also told her humorous incidents about his partner, the redoubtable Jackson. It would have made a great movie, even if it was only partially true.

He was good, no doubt about it, but so was she. The same experience that got him talking had taught her to recognize a carefully edited, laundered version when she heard one.

But that just made it more interesting.

She always learned as much from what wasn't said as she did from what was. Actually, she learned more. The trick, she had discovered early in the game, was to hear what the person meant, rather than what he or she said. It was easier with women, because almost all of them shared emotions as well as events. Most men spoke from their head, protecting their hearts with layers of logic and carefully objective opinions.

Nick had mastered the art of appearing open while revealing exactly what and how much he wanted—which wasn't a heck of a lot.

It hadn't mattered.

She merely affirmed what she had already suspected. He was a cop right down to his bones. It didn't matter that he was a detective and wore civvies instead of a uniform, he was still a cop. He could talk all night about how much safer it was than being on patrol, but he still put his life on the line every time he reported to work. Most of the time he dealt with sleazy human slime. He was idealistic enough to believe in justice, in the power of one person to right a wrong; he was human enough to be discouraged by the judicial system.

Nick was close to his family and saw them as often as he could. There had been women in his life, but there was no one now. He had never been married, and if his tone of voice was any indication, he wouldn't ever be. He obviously didn't think that cops had much to offer the home-and-hearth scene. He also had a bone-deep protective streak a mile wide, and he loved his partner.

Of course, being a male, he hadn't said any of those things. But just the same, they were true.

Marcy stepped back to the window and perched on the wide sill, giving a last tug to her laces, still thinking about Nick.

Since their discussion after leaving Zelda's kitchen two days ago, the tension between them had been thick enough

to slice with a machete. No, that wasn't exactly true, she
reflected, her eyes narrowing in thought. She was the only
one who seemed to be feeling the pressure. As far as Nick
was concerned, all the necessary explanations had been
made: he had not been trying to use her, he'd simply
wanted to clarify things before they became lovers. Then
he had gone a step further, assuring her that he was healthy
as a horse and offering to show her his most recent blood-
donor card.

Her temper obviously didn't faze the man, she thought
dryly. He knew he had infuriated her. Since an almost
frightening intelligence gleamed in his dark eyes and his
mind worked with the speed of a high-tech computer, he
was too smart not to know. But that hadn't stopped him.
Hadn't even slowed him down. For every step she retreated, he moved forward two, watching her like some
damn cat.

Why was he being so pushy, she brooded, watching a
gust of wind scatter more leaves around the yard. A man
with a mind like that should realize that she didn't like being pressured, didn't like feeling trapped and intimidated.

He did know it.

Her eyes widened at the thought. He knew exactly what
he was doing, damn his arrogant hide. And because he was
as aggressive as he was intelligent—and he knew if he gave
her an inch she'd retreat a mile—he never let up the pressure. Not even for a nanosecond.

Indignation narrowing her eyes, Marcy pulled the
sweatshirt over her head and tugged it down around her
hips before she tied her hair back on her nape with a small
scarf. Seconds later, she turned off the light and slipped
down the hall. This time she was going out the front door
and leaving it unlocked so she could get back in without
raising the dead.

Closing the door behind her, Marcy cast a considering glance at the sky. Thirty or forty minutes at the outside, she decided. The warm wind would bluster, but it would be at least that long before the rain came.

This was the last of her midnight flits, she promised herself, trotting down the familiar road. And this time she was not investigating weird cries or warnings—she realized they had been purely a figment of her imagination. Although, she thought, absently slowing her pace, Zelda's account of the screams she'd heard had been chilling, too close for comfort to the memory of her own imagined cries.

No, Marcy told herself firmly, she was not going to get sidetracked again. She was simply doing what she always did when researching a location, taking its emotional temperature at least several times—both in daylight and darkness. And if her sales figures were an indication of success, then her policy was right on target.

It was a good thing that night held no terrors for her, Marcy reflected, picking up speed. On the contrary. It was her favorite time, when darkness concealed the reality of modern civilization, when one could look at shadows and see images of the past.

Exhilaration, coupled with a sense of restless energy, gave her a heady sense of well-being. Sprinting down the road, she savored the air laden with moisture, the gathering sense of expectancy that always preceded a storm. As she ran, yesterday's conversation with Nick replayed itself in her head.

"You don't believe in ghosts," she had reminded him for the thousandth time. "You've told me that often, so why are you helping me when I interview people and go out to the old house?"

"Is that what I'm doing?"

"Nick."

He shrugged. "Just stubborn, I guess."

"I'm asking you a serious question."

"I'm giving you a serious answer. When I start something, I finish it."

She gave him an exasperated glance. "Perseverance is usually good for a few gold stars, but in this case it doesn't make sense."

His dark gaze held hers. "It does as long as you're still involved. I told you, Marcy, I'm in this for as long as you are. Besides, I'm your cold voice of reason, remember?"

"Did anyone ever tell you that you're pigheaded?"

"Yep."

"Uh, Nick?"

"Umm?"

"About Zelda? Do you think she really has any psychic ability?"

He grinned. "About as much as a road bump."

"You'd break her heart if you told her that."

"I'm not planning to. I think she's having the time of her life, and that's fine with me. I don't care how weird she gets, as long as she doesn't get you involved," he said deliberately.

"Give me a little credit, okay? Besides, what harm could she do?"

"Drag you off to that creaking wreck and hold a séance, for starters."

Marcy slanted a look up at him. "And if she did? Would it be so bad? She really believes it will help."

Nick's amusement faded, so did his tolerance. Swearing softly, he said, "Sure. Help the place fall down around your ears. I'll give you fair warning, lady, if you're even thinking of doing something that crazy, I'll hog-tie you."

"Nick!"

He scowled at her.

"Did I say I was? Well . . . did I?"

"No. But that doesn't mean a damn thing. You don't tell me about a lot of things that you do."

Well, he was right about that, Marcy reflected, slowing down as she veered into the rutted path. A prime example of that was her present expedition. You might say it was a declaration of independence. Of course, if all went well, he'd never even know about it, but if for some reason he did find out, he'd get the message loud and clear. That Marcy O'Bannon was a professional. She was independent. And she didn't ask anyone for permission to do her job.

She came to a stop and looked around, wishing for something larger and less prickly than a cactus to lean against while she caught her breath. She was getting tired of trudging up that hill, she admitted silently, especially in the dark. Somehow it didn't seem so steep when Nick was along. But the view at the top compensated for the climb, for the potential treachery of the small rocks underfoot, for the lack of a path in the wiry scrub brush.

Sighing, she took one step, then another, and was almost halfway up the slope when a gust of warm air made her stagger. It could be worse, she told herself, grabbing a scraggy bush for support as she brushed a handful of hair back from her face. At least she had the advantage of a tailwind.

Marcy reached the crest with a sound that was somewhere between a sigh and a gasp, stopping as she always did to look down at the mansion. The first sight of it always tugged at her imagination, and with a fleeting sense of guilt she admitted that she was glad Nick wasn't there.

The house brought out the romantic in her—the avowed, unadulterated, flaming romantic—and she didn't want the fire doused by Nick's estimations of how long it would be before the walls crumpled and the floors gave in. Nick called himself a realist, Marcy mused, squinting when a flurry of wind kicked up a cloud of dust. He was that all right.

What he needed, she decided as she started down the hill at a trot, was a touch of childlike wonder in his life, a bit of magic to counteract the darkness. From out of nowhere the thought came to her that Nick would make a very good father, protective and firm, but loving. She grinned as she skidded to a stop. It would be interesting to hear him explain the tooth fairy to a wide-eyed child.

Putting aside the thought of Nick for the time being, Marcy approached the house. She ambled to the back, tentatively touching the sagging wooden rail on the porch, running her fingers along the weathered boards and scraping at the peeling paint. She sat on the bottom step, gingerly testing its strength with a slight bounce, then leaned back, resting her elbows on the stair above.

Freedom, she thought with a slight grin. There was nothing like it. Nick would have drawn a circle twenty feet out from the house and ordered her not to cross it.

Marcy looked out across the small valley, mentally picturing an Indian village, populated by farmers and hunters—as were most of the California Indians—rather than warriors. Rectangular houses had been made from large cottonwood logs and covered with mud, she recalled, so that pretty much eliminated romantic images of tepees and camp fires. All in all it had probably been a peaceful valley, and prosperous. At least until the white man had come.

Considering the inevitable changes wrought by time and man, Marcy glanced around idly, her gaze coming to rest on several panes of glass level with the ground. They were small and even dirtier than the other windows. They were also behind several scraggly bushes, which probably accounted for the fact that she hadn't noticed them earlier. Undoubtedly they led to a full basement, the kind so common in Victorian houses.

She got up and walked over to the nearest one, eyeing it with rising excitement. It was small, very small. There was no way that a large man, someone like Nick for example, could get through it. Then again, she reflected, a large man, especially one like Nick, probably wouldn't want to.

A grin of anticipation lit her face. That left it, relatively speaking, wide open for someone small, easily tempted and without a cop's scruples when it came to breaking and entering an abandoned house.

Without giving the ethics of trespassing another thought, she dropped to her knees, took a tissue from her pocket and scrubbed at the window. "Damn!" She poked a finger through the frayed tissue just as a slash of lightning pierced the sky, illuminating the area. The dirt, baked on the glass by the desert sun, had the unforgiving texture of plaster.

Marcy sat back on her heels and scowled at the window. She brushed her hair out of her eyes, impatiently retying it with her scarf as thunder rumbled in the distance. Rocking to her knees again, she braced her hands under the sash and pushed.

"Come on," she muttered, "come *on*. You either do it the easy way or I get a rock." She inched forward to get more leverage and mumbled a heartfelt curse when her left knee came to rest on something that bit painfully into her sensitive skin.

Marcy reached down to remove it and for the second time in a week, all hell broke loose.

Lightning broke overhead in a sulfurous explosion, just as a shrill scream crackled through the air in a piercing wail.

"Run ... run ... ruuun!"

Nick looked at the illuminated numbers of the bedside clock and groaned. Twelve-thirty. It was going to be a long night.

Thunder grumbled in the distance as he shifted carefully, trying not to jostle his aching leg. The pain was the result of too much kneeling while he trimmed the bushes in Cristobel's backyard. It was also his own fault. He had felt a warning twinge about halfway around the sizable yard, but a combination of frustration and ego kept him at the task until he'd finished. That and the fact that Marcy had been working with him. He hadn't wanted her anxious green eyes zeroing in on his knee, and he didn't want her treating him like an invalid.

He wanted a lot of things from Marcy O'Bannon, he told himself, folding his hands behind his head and staring at the shadows of the ceiling.

None of them was pity.

He wanted her teasing laughter and enthusiasm directed at him. That was for starters. He needed the kind of sunlight that was so essentially a part of Marcy in his life. He sat up abruptly and lowered his feet to the floor. After that, he told himself as he headed for the medicine cabinet, he wanted her gorgeous eyes looking at him with something besides concern. A steady dose of awareness would do to begin with, he reflected, washing down a couple of aspirin with a glass of water. The same wary, appreciative, speculative look that he had detected a few times when he'd glanced up and caught her gaze on him.

Yeah, awareness would do just fine.

And desire. Definitely desire. He wanted to look into her eyes and see the heat flickering there, to know that she was as caught up in it as he was. That she wanted him every bit as much as he wanted her.

Nick paced back into the bedroom and opened the window a notch, remaining there to watch the wind agitate the leaves on the eucalyptus tree. The air was heavy with rain, the breeze sultry. He had stripped down to his cotton briefs and he was still hot. It would cool off in a while, he promised himself, even as he admitted that the change in temperature wouldn't help him. His heat had little to do with the weather and a lot to do with Marcy O'Bannon of the Santa Barbara O'Bannons.

Desire, he reminded himself. It would surprise her at first. She was so damned sure she had a handle on this mess, on him. She had it all blocked out, just like one of her outlines: they would find the nonexistent ghost, say a polite goodbye, she'd write a story and he'd go back to work. The end. Over. Kaput.

Surprise her? Oh, yeah. It would knock her on her sweet little tush.

For a man who rarely indulged in fantasies, he wasn't doing too bad, he decided with a wry grin. And next? He wanted her in his arms, pressing her sleek body against his, opening her mouth for his kisses. He wanted her hungry. For him.

Not bad at all, he decided, his smile broadening. He was on a roll. While he was at it, he wanted her tearing off his clothes and tugging him to the nearest bed. He had already decided that she would make love the way she fought—throwing herself into it headlong and damning the consequences. That's exactly how he wanted her, making demands, taking as much pleasure as she gave.

He turned back to the bed, wincing as the sudden movement shot pain up his knee. Dropping down on the mattress, he looked first at the clock then the telephone.

All right, Stoner, face it, you're still worried, it still doesn't feel right. You can play this little fantasy game for the rest of the night, or you can do something about the problem. The little voice isn't going away. In fact, it's getting louder all the time.

He picked up the receiver and poked out a seven-digit number. After the fourth ring an irritable voice said, "This better be good."

Nick grinned. "Hey, how's it going?"

"Do you know what time it is?"

"Yep. Got a clock right here."

"I'm busy," Jackson told him. "Catch me later."

Nick heard a feminine whisper mixed with the rumble of his partner's voice. "Tell the lady I'm sorry."

"What about me?"

"What the hell," he said expansively, "if you want 'em, you've got my apologies."

"You're all heart. Do you feel bad enough to hang up?"

"No."

Jackson was silent for a long moment. "What's up?" he asked softly.

Hesitating, Nick finally said, "I'm not sure. Maybe nothing, but I've got a feeling . . ."

"Oh, hell, you're listening to that little voice again."

"Yeah." Nick nodded. "And I don't like what it's saying."

"Don't blame you, partner. It always says the same thing. Trouble. You sure it's not the pain pills talking?"

"I tossed them out a week ago."

This time there was no hesitation. "I can be there in an hour."

"No. That's not why I called. I need some information."

"That's it? You called me at . . ."

Nick checked the clock. "Twelve thirty-seven," he said helpfully.

"—twelve-thirty-seven to tell me you want some—"

"Information. Right."

"You couldn't have called in the morning?"

"I wanted to make sure I got you."

Jackson groaned. "All right, what? *What?* What's so important?"

"There's an old abandoned house on the outskirts of town. Everyone around here calls it the Mulroony place. I want to know if any of the drug people are interested in it."

"You think they should be?"

"I don't know. I don't know one damn thing for sure. It's a possibility. We're close enough to the border to spit over it, so it could be. I just have this—"

"Feeling, I know. I'll check and get back with you tomorrow or the next day. Early as I can. Anything else?"

"No. Unless you know of a good ghost buster."

Jackson didn't say anything for a full ten seconds. "What the hell are you doing over there?" he finally asked in a neutral voice.

"It's a long story."

"You're not supposed to be checking out haunted houses," Jackson reminded him. "You're on sick leave."

"My knee never lets me forget it."

"Just don't mess it up any more," he ordered. "They've got me working with Curtis, and his rancid pipe is driving me nuts."

"Right. Hey, Jackson?"

"Yeah?"

"I owe you one."

"Hell, you owe me a whole bunch of them. Now hang up and let me—"

"Get back to what you were doing. Talk to you tomorrow."

Nick's smile faded when he cradled the receiver. He reached for his pants. Before tomorrow came he had a long night to get through, and it wasn't going to pass fast enough in bed.

He pulled on his jeans and padded barefoot down the hall into the kitchen. The room was a perfect reflection of Cristobel's personality, he decided as he turned on the lights. Pale yellow walls and sparkling white trim brought sunlight into the room even on the dreariest day. Baskets of colorful silk flowers brightened it even more. She had made it the hub of the house, comfortable and inviting. Visitors were usually seated at the glass-topped table, basking in their warm welcome long before they noticed the underlying efficiency of the room.

He had a strong hunch that Marcy's place was much the same, well organized for her particular needs and brimming with the same effortless charm. Nick measured some coffee into the glass pot and plugged it in. The two women were a lot alike, he realized with a sense of surprise. Bold and bright, friendly to a fault, inquisitive as a litter of pups, and neither had a shred of self-preservation. Hell, he had seen Cristobel's mugger size her up as a victim from half a block away. What had she done as the slimeball approached? Smiled and inquired about his health, said he looked pale.

Marcy would probably have done the same thing, he reflected in disgust, pouring a mug of coffee. She had no more sense of danger than a kitten. Less. Add to that the fact that she preferred to travel around at night like a damned vampire, and you had nothing but trouble.

He walked over to the window, automatically checking the lock before he took a swallow of coffee. She hadn't liked it when he told her to stop her nocturnal jaunts, he recalled with a wince, moving to test the doorknob. That was putting it mildly—she'd reared up like a spitting cat.

Marcy was accustomed to being on her own. Free. She didn't like having her wings clipped.

He shrugged. She'd get used to it in time. He didn't care how mad she was, as long as she was safe.

Maybe he was being too cautious. Maybe he wasn't. Maybe the old house was safe. Maybe it wasn't. Until he knew for sure the place was safe, he wasn't letting her run any risks. Until he knew, there was just an off chance that she could run smack into a drug dealer or worse out there. Of course, knowing Marcy, she'd probably traipse up to him, whip out her notebook and ask for an interview.

Nick wandered into the dining room, checking locks as he went, feeling a bit like the lord of the castle. It was a sensation he had never had at his condo, but one he rather liked. The difference, he knew, was that Marcy was asleep in her room, vulnerable, trusting, relying on him to protect her. It made him feel primitive, possessive.

And horny as hell.

A real lord of the castle had one major advantage, Nick reminded himself. His woman would be in his bed. After securing the house, he would slide in next to her, take her in his arms and pleasure her until they both went wild.

Nick swore as his body hardened at the thought. He had no right to go into Marcy's room. Or her bed. Not yet.

But soon, he promised himself.

Very soon.

Nick's eyes had adjusted to the darkness, and he moved silently through the house without turning on the lights. Telling himself that sentry duty was overdoing things a bit,

he did it anyway. Even knowing that he had secured all the
locks before he'd gone to bed, he checked again. It was an
automatic reflex learned on the job. Check and double
check. Take nothing for granted. He circled the room and
found exactly what he expected to find: locks and bolts in
place.

Until he tried the door.

The knob turned easily in his hand and the solid oak
door swung toward him without a sound from its well-
oiled hinges. One glance assured him that the lock had not
been tampered with, no one had tried to open it from the
outside.

"Damn it to hell!"

An urge to do something violent raged through Nick,
followed by a blend of fury and fear. The combination sent
adrenaline pumping through his body. He glared at the
door, torn between astonished disbelief and rage.

"She's done it again!"

He flexed his fingers and took a deep breath, just man-
aging not to slam his fist through the door. This time there
was no doubt about it. She was asking for trouble, and if
she hadn't already found it, he'd give her plenty.

As soon as he had her safe, he was going to throttle her!

Six

Nick exploded through the door, fighting a cold chill that threatened to paralyze him. Marcy was out there. In the dark. Defenseless. Alone at a time when the rats, both the four- and two-legged varieties, came out of their holes. He vaulted the porch rail, skidding when his feet hit the lush grass surrounding the house.

The pain radiating from his knee was intense. Ignoring it, he broke into a ground-covering jog, visualizing the road ahead. It would take ten minutes to reach the Mulroony place. Ten minutes of hard running on two good legs, he amended grimly. Triple that with a bad knee and... He looked down.

Bare feet.

Cold logic told him that between cactus thorns and sharp rocks he wouldn't get ten feet without shoes once he left the protection of the lawn.

Swearing softly, inventively and with great feeling, Nick stopped. One minute, he promised himself. Sixty seconds or less he'd be back on her track.

But he hadn't counted on the rain.

Lightning blossomed in the black sky, shaping itself into stark fingers of fire. At the same time a deafening clap of thunder shook the ground.

And the sky opened up.

Half blinded by the searing light and pelting rain, Nick turned back to the house, moving swiftly even while he tried to spare his knee. Before he had gone two feet, he was drenched. The rain came down in sheets, cold as the stinging wind that carried it. Knowing that Marcy was bound to be as wet and chilled as he was, he kept moving, swearing when he slipped on the slick grass. Seconds later he leaped onto the walk leading to the stairs, taking the impact with his good leg.

Thunder jolted and blinding streaks of lightning snarled across the sky, leaving him groping in the utter darkness that followed. Three steps away from the porch he was broadsided by a force that knocked him to the ground.

Instinctively Nick rolled, reaching out to grab his attacker. His hand closed on a sodden jacket. When he hauled it closer, his opponent jerked and aimed a lethal kick at him before trying to squirm away. If he yelled, the sound was lost beneath the noise of hammering rain. Nick yanked savagely on the jacket and rolled again, letting the body beneath him take his full weight.

Swearing, still half blinded, he delivered a chopping blow to the fist stabbing something in his bare shoulder. Not a knife, he realized at a subconscious level. Nothing lethal, but pointed enough to hurt like hell.

The rain didn't let up. If anything, it came down harder. Nick shook his head and deliberately kept his full weight on the punk beneath him. That's all he was, he had realized with a sense of shock when he'd landed on him. A kid, as slippery as an eel but a long way away from having the bulk and strength of a man. Nick didn't ease up; kids could be just as vicious, especially if they were strung out on drugs.

He stayed where he was, thinking of his options. He wanted his cuffs, a rope, his gun and a light. Not necessarily in that order. Cristobel's neighborhood didn't come equipped with anything as fancy as streetlights, and it was so dark he couldn't even make out the bulk of the house, much less the punk.

A fierce urgency drove him. Marcy. Curious and rash, she could be anywhere. And she was too small, too soft to handle the kind of trouble that was always around, just waiting for a victim. Nick grabbed a handful of wet material and twisted. He smiled grimly as the kid writhed and kicked. He was in no mood to play games with an apprentice mugger, even one who had bungled things as badly as this one had.

Nick sat up, straddling the youth, running his hand over the sodden, bunched up clothes, making no effort to be gentle. He wasn't feeling indulgent, especially when he thought how the incident could have ended if the punk had run into Marcy instead of him.

The kid bucked and tried to roll away. Nick tightened the grip of his knees and held him in the vice of his legs. With grim intent, he wrapped his hand around the punk's neck. Just as his fingers started squeezing, he realized several things.

The kid's neck was slim.

And smooth.

And soft.

Woman soft.

Swearing with a rage and volume that was lost in the wind, Nick moved his other hand with unerring accuracy to verify that he was dealing with a woman. He was. And he knew with absolute certainty which one. There was only one woman crazy enough to be running around in this weather.

Not just *a* woman.

Not just *any* woman.

His woman.

"Damn it to hell!" His hands dropped as if they had been burned. Cursing the darkness, the wind and the rain, Nick moved, sitting back on his heels. He shifted again when his knee protested, putting his weight on his good leg. There'd be hell to pay with that knee, he thought absently. But that was later. Right now he had a cold, wet and terrified woman to soothe. Even if she had brought it all on herself.

At the thought, his anger flared again. He could have throttled her. He had been within an inch of doing just that. She was lucky she wasn't worse off. Cold and wet was small potatoes compared to dead. His hands settled on her shoulders just as a full-bodied, thoroughly outraged feminine shriek tore through the air.

"Marcy, you're okay, honey."

Another hair-raising scream was his answer.

"Marcy, you're all right!" He pulled her up on her knees into his arms, momentarily forgetting his rage. God, she was so soft, so right. His arms tightened, holding her closer.

Lightning cracked and fizzed overhead, lighting the yard like a football field. Marcy blinked and leaned back, peering up through the torrent of rain. "Nick?"

"You were thinking it might be someone else?" He had to shout to be heard over the downpour. Adrenaline was still pouring through his bloodstream, and he released her until he could get it under control. Another forceful reminder from his knee persuaded him to continue the conversation in the house.

He briefly closed his eyes, took a ragged breath, then heaved himself to his feet. Holding out his hand, he said, "Come on, sweetheart, let's get inside."

Marcy sat back on her heels and seemed to consider his carefully controlled voice. Apparently deciding she didn't want to deal with it, she put her hand in his, allowing him to pull her from the saturated grass. She gave him a smile almost as brilliant as the forked lightning. "It's raining!"

"Marcy," he said definitely, "we're not going to start talking about the storm again, especially while we're standing in the middle of the damn thing." He glanced upward at the lightning leapfrogging through the sky, then hustled her toward the house. "Hurry, that stuff's getting too close for comfort." When she seemed about to say something, he shook his head. *"Now!"*

Marcy trotted obediently beside him, coming to a stop when they reached the sanctuary of the porch. Whirling to face him, she demanded, "What on earth are you doing out here without a shirt? And shoes? That's just asking for a cold!"

Speechless, Nick stared at her. The woman was going to drive him right over the edge. She looked as if she'd fallen in a damn river, had come within an inch of being strangled on the front lawn, and all she could think of was his missing shirt. He silently opened the door and nudged her through, closing it behind him. They exchanged scowls, dripping on the entryway tile until he finally said, "You don't look any warmer or drier than I do. What's your excuse?"

Marcy glanced down at her waterlogged clothes then shrugged. "I miscalculated." She took a second survey. "Nick, you ruined my sweatshirt! Look."

Nick looked. The heavy cotton shirt was torn along the shoulder seam and below the arm. The sleeve was almost severed. Dry, the shirt would have fallen to her waist. Only the fact that it was sodden and clinging to her body kept it up.

"That's one of the risks you take when you attack people in the dark," he said dryly.

"Attack?" Marcy looked bewildered. "I didn't attack you! I bumped into you."

"If that's the case, you were moving at one hell of a speed."

"I suppose I was. I was . . . running."

Nick stiffened, as much at the word as her evasive tone. "From what?" he asked grimly.

She looked at him indignantly. "For heaven's sake! Why couldn't I be running just to be running? For the exercise," she added as an afterthought.

"You could have been," he agreed in an even voice, "but you weren't. Something happened while you were out, didn't it?"

"Nick—"

"Something that scared you."

Marcy stared at him.

"What was it?"

Stubborn silence was her only answer.

"Okay," he said quietly. "You don't have to tell me." He waited until she gave him a relieved smile and added, "Not now. After you take a hot shower and get in some warm clothes will be fine. Say in about twenty minutes."

When she swung around and headed for her room, the stubborn set of her shoulders warned him. "Marcy," he said even more gently, "if you're not here, I'm coming to get you."

Twenty-five minutes later Marcy sat in the living room, sipping a cup of hot chocolate, listening to the storm rage outside. She was curled up in the corner of the brown leather sofa, wearing a pale yellow wraparound robe with the sash tied firmly at her waist. The bottom edge was tucked under her bare feet. As it dried, her hair fell in long, unruly waves around her shoulders and down her back.

Nick, in her opinion was sitting far too close. Instead of taking the chair facing the couch, he had opted to sprawl next to her, so close that his shoulders and thighs brushed hers when either of them moved. After the night she'd had, the situation was unnerving.

It was also fascinating. And carried an element of risk that Marcy simply couldn't resist. There was something addictive about playing with fire, especially when there was no real danger of getting burned. She could definitely understand a moth's attraction to flame. The only problem with that setup was the moth didn't know when to quit.

If wasn't as if she needed the physical contact to be aware of him, Marcy reflected, still optimistic enough to believe that she could deal with the situation—and Nick Stoner. Women would always react to him. Nick had what Zelda called a strong masculine aura. In layman's terms, that meant he was overwhelming.

Yes, indeed, that he was.

And she was curious.

She had experienced his strength twice now—regrettably, both times in hand-to-hand combat—a third time if she counted the day he'd swept her off the boulder into his arms. Yes, she decided after another sip of chocolate, that was definitely worth counting. Nick was a physical man, honed down to muscle and sinew, a sleek, powerful animal. What was more, he was intelligent enough to know exactly how to use his strength.

Turning so the arm of the couch was at her back, Marcy wasn't surprised when Nick calmly reached out and draped her legs across his thighs. When the edges of her robe parted to just above her knees, he eyed the length of bare leg with masculine satisfaction. Looking like a man who had just been seated at a banquet table, he smoothed one large hand from her ankle to thigh, parting the robe even more.

Marcy smacked his hand and primly pulled the material together, covering her knees. "Watch it, buster. I happen to know a very protective cop. One word from me and you're dead meat."

Nick grinned and settled for resting one hand on her covered thigh. With the other one he absently traced the curve of her bare leg from ankle to knee.

Marcy blinked thoughtfully at his absorbed profile. Either the business tonight had lowered the floodgates or Nick was allowing her to see a part of him that he had been concealing. He was touching, stroking, seeming to absorb the essence of her through his rough fingertips. And he had all the earmarks of becoming more than a tad possessive.

At least he was dressed, she reflected, taking what comfort she could from the situation. The problem was, his dark sweats and black T-shirt gave him a menacing air, like a modern-day pirate.

It was as sexy as all get-out.

Thinking that he was also a double handful of trouble, Marcy shivered when his fingers brushed the back of her knee. There was a distinct possibility that she had overestimated her ability to deal with Nick, she speculated. She was tired, her nerves were frayed, her resistance was definitely down, and he sat there like a contented cat waiting for his next meal.

She had a strong hunch she knew what was on the menu.

Marcy set her cup down with a blink. Nick looked at her with raised brows. Waiting. Just waiting. The man was going to drive her crazy.

"I don't know what all the fuss is about," she told him again, an aggrieved note entering her voice in spite of herself. "I told you the other day that I wasn't making any more promises. If I wanted to go walking at three in the morning, I'd do it."

He nodded. "So you did. What I want to know is what happened while you were out tonight?"

"You keep asking me that," she said, scowling at him.

"Yep." He nodded again. "I do. It's the cop in me. I ask a lot of questions."

"Nothing happened."

He waited, touching her ankle with his finger, smiling when she shivered.

"Nothing at all," Marcy insisted. It was a passive torture technique, she decided. Probably something he learned at the police academy.

"Nothing important."

Nick raised her hand to his mouth, kissing the tip of each finger.

"It was silly," she said weakly.

He gave her an encouraging glance.

"You'll think I'm crazy."

He shook his head, looking at her thoughtfully. "I doubt it. I think you're reckless and too trusting. And sometimes you scare the hell out of me, but you're smart, and beneath all of that ingenuous charm you're level-headed. You're not silly, and you're not crazy."

"You think I'm charming?" she asked, pleased and willing to be distracted.

Nick's hand closed around her ankle. "I think you're a lot of things, but we'll discuss them all later. Right now, I want you to tell me what scared you."

"I went to the old house," she said abruptly. "No, you don't have to bristle like that. I didn't run into a ring of white slavers. It was just an old house, deserted and quiet. I sat on the back steps and—" she gave a small shrug "—dreamed a little. Thought about how I'd approach the story. Then I noticed the basement windows."

Nick's hand tightened around her ankle. "Basement," he repeated in a neutral tone.

"Did you know they were there?" She eyed him suspiciously. "I suppose you were keeping quiet about them so I wouldn't be tempted to explore?" When he shook his head, she gave his arm a quick pat. "Oh, well, those ugly bushes were in front of them, so they were easy to miss," she comforted. "Anyway, I noticed the windows."

"And were you?"

"Was I what?" she asked blankly.

"Tempted."

She gave a sudden gurgle of laughter. "Of course."

"Oh, God."

"I tried to clean one off, but I couldn't. I needed a sandblaster instead of a tissue."

He closed his eyes. "And then?"

"I tried to open it, of course."

"Dammit, Marcy, don't you know that's—"

"Trespassing." She nodded. "Or breaking and entering. I'm not sure what the difference is. It's probably a moot point, anyway, because there's no one there to trespass on. Or against. Whatever. Besides, who would complain? After all, it's just an empty, old—"

"So did you?"

"Did I what?"

"Dammit, woman," Nick exploded, "can't you follow a simple conversation? Did you get in the place?"

"Oh, that. No. I couldn't open the window."

"I'm surprised you let that stop you," he muttered.

"Well, I was going to look for a rock—"

Nick groaned.

"—but before I could find one..." Her voice faded away.

With one easy motion, Nick scooped her to his lap, repeating, "Before you could find—" He stopped as if he had run into a glass wall, his hand working down her spine to her lush derriere and back to her shoulders to affirm his sudden realization. She didn't have a thing on beneath the yellow robe.

She had been sitting there calmly, sipping hot chocolate, almost in his arms, practically naked as a jaybird! He gave a silent groan, reminding himself that she had had a rough evening, that he was supposed to be protecting her. He could not rip off her robe and make wild, erotic love to her on Cristobel's couch. At least not right now.

His sudden tension communicated itself to Marcy, and the shadowy dread left her eyes. Touching his arm, she asked, "What's the matter?"

Nick shook his head. "Nothing." Clearing his throat, he forced himself back to where they had been before he'd discovered he had a seminaked woman in his arms. "You were—uh—looking for a rock. Then what?"

The look was back in her eyes, so he tightened his grasp. "Get it over with," he said grimly. "Tell me."

She took a deep breath. "I heard the screams again." She said the words so hastily, it took Nick a few seconds to absorb them.

"Screams? The same kind that Zelda heard?"

Marcy shuddered and nodded. "They were... frightening," she said quietly, in what was obviously a massive understatement. She turned in his arms and looked up. "Nick, no human voice made those sounds I heard."

His large hands soothed her shoulders, but his gaze was preoccupied, as if he were listening intently to an inner voice. "Again," he murmured. "You said you heard them again."

She nodded, nestling against his broad chest. "The first time we walked out to the house I heard them." She smiled. "During my twelve-and-a-half-minute grace period."

Nick's arms tightened convulsively around her, almost stopping her breathing. "Damn it all, why didn't you say something then?" he roared.

Marcy drew as far away from him as she could. It wasn't far enough to suit her. She was still on his lap with his arm across her thighs, his hand cupping her hip. "Will... you...stop...swearing at me," she said between clenched teeth. "And while you're at it, stop shouting. I understand basic English, and I'm not deaf."

In a calmer voice she said, "I didn't say anything to you that day because the sound was so faint I wasn't actually sure I heard something. I finally wrote it off as an overactive imagination and put it out of my mind."

His eyes narrowed. "Did you really forget about it, or did you just put it aside?" He held up a hand to stop another outburst. "I'm not being deliberately aggravating," he assured her, grinning when she eyed him skeptically. He couldn't help it. She looked like a tousled, indignant kitten. "And I'm not doubting your word. I'm trying to understand your frame of mind. Were you genuinely convinced you heard nothing and put it out of your mind, or did you *try* to forget it because it seemed the logical thing to do?''

"Thereby leaving myself open to a panic attack the first time I heard the wind moaning?" Marcy settled back against him, fitting her head in the hollow of his shoulder.

She considered the question thoughtfully, "It's a cop's question, but a fair one. I truly believed I'd made a mistake. I know from personal experience that writers sometimes go off half-cocked when their imaginations take over, and I don't allow myself to function in la-la land. In spite of my imagination, I deal with reality."

She tilted her head back and gave him a quick smile. "I can be philosophical at times. And logical. I wrote it off," she said firmly. "Although I will admit to a shock when Zelda talked about hearing screams. Her description was very close to what I *thought* I had heard."

"And after she talked about it? Did you start thinking that maybe you really had heard something?" Wondering if he was making sense, Nick gazed down at the gaping neck of Marcy's robe, at the tantalizing curve of her breast. The woman was going to drive him crazy. Flat-out nuts.

Marcy shook her head. "Nope." She chuckled sleepily. "I gave it about five seconds of thought, but Zelda isn't exactly my idea of a rock-solid witness, so it never occurred to me to go back over that ground. As far as I was concerned, it was settled."

Nick's arm tightened around her waist. "You said you heard the voice. Exactly what did you hear? I want to know it all, from beginning to end."

Marcy told him, ending at the point where she bolted. When it said 'run,' I didn't hang around to ask questions.

I ran. Nick, you can't imagine that voice," she said, with a shudder. "It sounded insane. But most of all, it sounded . . . inhuman."

She waited, knowing that he would have a few pointed comments to make. He always did. You would think he was the writer—the man was never at a loss for words. After several minutes of silence passed, she nudged him. "Nick?"

"Hmm?" His hand worked down her thigh to cup her knee.

"What are we going to do about it?"

"About what?"

She heaved a sigh. "The voice. The thing, whatever it is."

"Nothing." His tone told her the matter wasn't negotiable. "At least, not now." Nick's warm hand stilled her restless fingers. "What's that?"

"This?" She handed him the object she had picked up from the table. It was a green-and-brown feather, eight or nine inches long. "I knelt on it when I was trying to open the basement window," she explained. "It hurt, and I reached for it just as the voice screamed. I didn't even realize I still had it in my hand until I got upstairs. I brought it down to show you."

"It's a good thing it isn't gray, or Zelda would be sure you brought a message from her guide," he said absently, tossing it aside.

Marcy cleared her throat. "Nick, I'm afraid that I—uh, might have used the quill end out there on the grass to try to stab you."

"You didn't puncture me," he said dryly. "But if it's any consolation, it hurt like hell. When I was in the shower, I noticed some choice bruises."

"Oh, no! Let me see." Marcy sat up and grabbed the hem of his shirt, pushing it up until she could see his chest. Her warm hands were all over him, patting and soothing the angry wounds. "I'm so sorry." She leaned closer and impulsively pressed her lips to a purplish mark almost hidden in the crisp dark hair several inches above his nipple.

"That does it," Nick said in a strangled voice.

"What?" Marcy jumped, her eyes widening in alarm when he groaned. *"What?"*

Nick slid his hands up her arms, stopping above her elbows, exerting just enough pressure to get her attention. When her gaze met his, he said tightly, "I'll tell you what. For just a few seconds, I want you to put Indians and ghosts out of your mind and look at me."

Marcy looked. At a man who was tired and exasperated. A man whose indulgence had been stretched to the limit. A man who had just decided to pull a slack rope taut. Oh, dear, she thought inadequately. She had indeed underestimated her ability to deal with Nick.

"What do you see, Marcy?"

"A good friend," she said stoutly, giving it her best shot, knowing that she lied through her teeth. What she saw was a red danger signal, a threat, a claim made the night Nick had pulled her through the front door.

"Wrong." He gave her a small shake. "A friend is someone you play checkers with. Look again."

Marcy looked. At a strong man's hunger. At an honest man's refusal to play games.

"What do you see, Marcy?" he asked again, laying her hands against his bare chest, holding them there.

She shivered at the touch of his crisp hair on her palms. "A man," she said faintly. A man who had lived in the dark too long, who needed sunlight in his life. Who needed the love of a good woman. Who knew how to protect but might never be vulnerable enough to love.

Love? Marcy wondered, half dazed by the thought. Who was talking about love? Hunger, undoubtedly; lust, maybe. Desire. Plain, old, simple sex. But love?

Marcy stopped. She had never been good at fooling herself, and this was no time to start. She didn't know what Nick was thinking, but she was dealing with love. Somehow, somewhere between all the battles, she had fallen in love with the impossible man!

Stunned by the revelation, she missed Nick's question.

"Marcy." His hands tightened on her wrists. "I asked what kind of a man?"

"A stubborn, arrogant, demanding, chauvinistic, thoroughly hopeless man," she said in exasperation. "One who doesn't know when to quit pushing." She bit back a grin, as the question in his black eyes became a gleam of outright speculation.

Her voice softened. "A beautiful, strong, caring man," she whispered, gently kneading his chest with her fingertips.

"One you're going to stay with for the next couple of weeks?" he asked, hope mingling with a touch of pure masculine satisfaction.

"Yes," she said simply, knowing that she had agreed to far more than a simple question.

Blinking, Nick said cautiously, "Yes?"

"Yes."

Nick slid down on the couch, carrying Marcy with him. "Do you know how scared I was tonight when I found the door open and knew that you were gone?" he demanded, crushing her close against him.

She shook her head. "I thought I'd be back before you woke up. If you did find out, I expected you to be mad, not scared."

His voice hardened. "If you ever pull a trick like that again—"

"Nick, this is a lousy time for a lecture." Marcy propped her elbows on his shoulders and looked down at him expectantly. Her eyes were level with his. She inched down and brushed her lips against his.

Nick inhaled sharply and sat up. He surged to his feet, taking her with him. "You're right," he muttered, shifting her higher in his arms. "But, tomorrow—" He stepped on his injured leg and winced.

"My room is closer," Marcy said hastily as he turned down the hall.

"You're right," he agreed. "It is." He didn't stop.

"I can walk, you know. You don't have to carry me." Marcy frowned up at him, anxiety momentarily overriding her initial surge of excitement. It wasn't every day a woman literally got carried away by a man, but someone had to use some common sense here!

The quick kiss that Nick gave her was hard and thoroughly possessive. She forgot all about being practical.

"Indulge me," he muttered, his dark eyes gleaming with anticipation. "For years I've fantasized about carrying a gorgeous redhead off to my bed."

Marcy sighed, entranced. "I do believe you're a closet romantic, Nick Stoner."

"There's another reason." He gave her a pirate's grin. "Part of my job is to serve and protect. And, sweetheart, the protection is in here."

Seven

Nick nudged the bedroom door open with his shoulder and carried Marcy in. He set her on her feet between the large picture window and the massive bed, keeping her in the circle of his arms.

The lamp at the far end of the hall cast a dim glow through the open door, and Marcy took a quick look around. With just a few books, and personal possessions, Nick had put his stamp on the room. She had a feeling that he did that wherever he went.

During the day the room had a sweeping view of the distant mountains, but right now the window was dark, pebbled with rain, a perfect screen for the jagged forks of light intermittently illuminating the sky. The storm was moving on, she noted subconsciously, balancing herself by clinging to Nick's shoulders.

"Don't move," he ordered against her lips, cradling her nape with one hand and sliding the other down to cup her buttock, pressing her firmly against him.

Move? Marcy dug her bare toes into the deeply piled rug, shivering when Nick's lips lightly brushed hers, then settled back with a distinctly possessive touch.

Move? Her arms curled around his neck as his words finally made an impression. Why would she do anything that crazy?

Nick kissed the same way he did everything else—with single-minded intensity, she decided, nestling closer and letting him take her weight. Lacing her fingers in his thick, dark hair, she smiled against his lips. Being the object of that kind of concentration made a woman feel feminine... and very sensual.

Even if she wasn't.

Even if she had an extremely limited and rather mediocre track record in that area.

Marcy's smile faded as quickly as it had come. It was replaced by an anxious frown.

"Do you know how long I've wanted you like this?" Nick groaned. He pressed his lips to the rapid pulse in her throat, his hands working down and stopping at the sash at her waist. "Since that first night."

"When I overwhelmed you with my fatal charm?" Marcy asked with sudden flippancy, burying her face against his chest and covering his hands with hers, stopping him.

"No, when you tried to kick me in the family jewels, then settled for a wrestling match. I knew you were my kind of woman. Come closer, Marcy. Feel what you do to me."

Typically, Nick didn't try to hide his need, she thought. He was as bluntly honest about that as he was everything else, but she was stunned to find herself dealing with a re-action that was as unexpected as it was unnerving.

His voice tightened, and his large hands turned to capture hers. "What's the matter, honey? Changed your mind?"

"Oh, Nick," she wailed softly, keeping her face pressed against him. "No. I want you, I really do. I want—" she waved an agitated hand "—this. But..."

"But, what?"

She sighed deeply into his chest.

"I'm here, babe. I'm listening." Nick wrapped his arms around her, just holding her.

Marcy lifted her head and looked up at him. It took just about all the courage she had. Lightning flickered in the distance, sending a brief shaft of light across his hard face. Nick was as taut as a drawn bow. She could feel the tension in his rigid frame, see it in his face, but he was in control. And he would be, she knew with absolute conviction, for as long as he needed to be.

"It's just been . . . a long time," she admitted, grasping the front of his shirt with a death grip. There was a limit to honesty, she thought, making a rapid decision. He didn't have to know just how very long it had been—or how infrequent. "I don't take these things lightly," she said in a rush, "and I'm not nearly as blasé about it as I thought I'd be."

Nick exhaled sharply, and she could feel the tension seeping out of him. "Don't stop now," he said wryly. "What's the bottom line here?"

Marcy swallowed. "That I'm pretty close to panic and talking about it isn't making it any easier. I'm horribly embarrassed."

Nick gave a shout of laughter and plucked her up into his arms. "Is that all?" he asked, swinging her around and settling her back on her feet.

"All?" Her eyes widened indignantly. "*All?* Nick, I'm twenty-seven years old, for heaven's sake! I ought to be able to handle this with a bit more . . . savoir faire."

Still grinning, he put a finger across his lips. "Hush a minute. I'm going to give you lesson number one in the Stoner all-purpose manual. Do you know what a man wants when he takes a woman to bed?"

Marcy shot him a resentful glance. That was exactly the problem. She didn't know. Not for sure. She had a natural fastidiousness that had kept her experience limited. And what she did have had not been with dangerous, sensual men like Nick, men who knew exactly what they wanted. The end result had been pretty much one-sided and had convinced her that someone had done a good job of hoodwinking the general public. If it were the kind of thing she'd write home about, she had decided, she definitely wouldn't bother.

She gave a sulky shrug. "You're just dying to tell me, so go ahead."

Nick laced his fingers in her wild mane of hair, sliding his thumbs along her jawline until her face tilted up to his. "A man doesn't want poise, savoir faire, or, God forbid, control in bed. He wants honesty."

Marcy blinked. "That's it?"

"That's it. Of course, honesty brings a few other things along with it."

Marcy frowned. She knew there was a hitch. "Like what?" she said suspiciously.

Nick grinned again. He couldn't help it. She looked like a ruffled kitten gearing up to pounce on a new toy: half wary, wholly intrigued. He turned her so she was facing the dim light in the hallway. He wanted—no, desperately needed—to see her expressive face.

"What else?" she demanded.

Nick shrugged. "Curiosity. Enthusiasm. Humor. Asking questions and paying attention to the answers."

Marcy blinked. She could do that. "What kind of questions?"

"Easy ones. Like this." His hands still cradling her face, he bent his head and kissed her, tasting her, savoring her instinctive response. When he lifted his head, he was breathing faster. "Did you like that?"

Marcy's lashes were dark shadows on her cheeks. She lifted them with an effort and cleared her throat. "Yes."

"Do you want me to do it again?"

She nodded. "Yes."

"The same way?"

Marcy thought about it and said, "Experiment a little."

This time the kiss was deeper, a bit rougher, and the tip of his tongue sought and found hers.

"Like that?" Nick muttered.

"Mmm, yes."

Exhaling sharply, Nick closed his eyes and fought for control. When he opened them, it was to find Marcy's inquisitive gaze on him.

"That's it," she demanded again. "You do something and ask if I like it? If I do, you do it again?"

"As simple as that," he assured her, wondering how long he was going to last. He was hard, had been since her first wide-eyed question. Hell, he was always hard around Marcy. Her barely leashed energy sizzled in the room, and whether she knew it or not, she was dying to try her feminine wiles and finely honed reporter's skills on him. And he knew from personal experience that no one could ask questions like Marcy O'Bannon.

He wondered if he'd make it through the night.

Looking at the speculation in her eyes, he knew he didn't care.

Marcy blinked. "Do you want to take off your shirt?" she asked politely.

Grateful for the dim light, Nick bit back a grin. "Will you do it?"

"Do you want me to?"

"Yes."

She took a deep breath. "Then I will."

"While you're at it," he said blandly, "you can take off anything else you want to."

Marcy barely heard him, so engrossed was she in the task she'd set for herself. She slid her hands beneath the knit shirt, testing his sleek skin, gliding her fingers over crisp hair and smoothly bunched muscles. Stepping closer, she rested her cheek against his chest and wrapped her arms around him, working her hands up his spine, brushing his shoulders and touching his nape.

Nick groaned.

"What?" Marcy jumped. "Did I hurt you?"

"No. Don't stop. You're doing fine. Wonderful." She was going to kill him. She didn't even have the shirt off yet, and he was ready to explode. He had expected her to pull it over his head with a quick tug, not plaster herself against him like a second skin and practically climb in with him.

"I guess I'd better get this off, huh?"

"Good idea," Nick said between clenched teeth. "Great."

"I don't want to hurt you," she mumbled. "You're sore where I stabbed you with the feather." Starting at the bottom again, she inserted her fingers under the hem and eased the shirt up, her palms skimming his rib cage. She stopped abruptly when her fingertips eased through a dusting of crisp hair and encountered his pebbled nipples. She grazed them tentatively with her nails.

Nick sucked in his breath.

"Do you like that?" Marcy slanted a quick glance up. Yes, he did. Her brows rose in pleased speculation. The whole thing seemed pretty straightforward so far. Maybe she was getting the hang of it.

"Yes."

"Want me to do it again?"

"Yes!"

She did, and smiled a very small, very feminine smile at his reaction. This wasn't as hard as she'd thought it was going to be. Things were looking up. A convulsive movement from Nick informed her that several things were looking up. It didn't really surprise her. Nick was a passionate, sensual man and with any luck at all, she had expected this reaction. Or at least, hoped for it.

What did surprise Marcy was the heated coil of tension twisting and building within her. Each time she touched Nick and felt his uncontrolled reaction, it grew stronger. It felt as if her nerves were simmering on the surface of her skin, and it left her restless and wanting more. A lot more.

"There!" Marcy gave a tug and pulled the shirt over his head. She tossed it aside and stared at him.

"What's the matter?" Concern roughened his voice.

Marcy shook her head. "Nothing."

"Something is. Why are you looking at me like that?"

"Because," she said slowly, "you're beautiful."

Nick cupped her face with his hands and shook his head. "No, if you want to see beauty, come over here and look in the mirror."

Marcy didn't budge. "I know it when I see it," she said stubbornly. "And I'm looking at it." Nick went without a shirt a good deal of the time, so she had frequently seen his sleek, muscular chest. But it was different, somehow, standing next to him in a near dark room and knowing that soon they wouldn't be standing at all, but lying on that huge bed.

The thought made her nervous, so she said brightly, "What's next?"

Nick bent his head and dropped a kiss on the tip of her nose. "Would you like me to take off your robe?"

Her eyes widened. "I don't have anything on under it."

"I know." The satisfaction in his voice surprised her. The anticipation she saw on his face stunned her.

Marcy took a deep breath. "I...think...so."

Nick didn't wait for her to consider the matter further. He wouldn't rush her, but he wouldn't give her a chance to change her mind, either. He loosened the tie at her small waist and let it fall to the floor. The edges of the robe slowly parted.

No, he wouldn't rush her, he told himself, grimly ignoring the painful tension in his loins. He wouldn't pounce and he wouldn't grab. Even if it killed him. And it just might. Some idiot—or idiots—had already done that and had convinced her that she lacked some essential sensual ingredient.

What Marcy needed was a patient man, a man who would let her discover the fire that sizzled through her, from her dark mane of hair to her pretty toes. And he was damn well going to be that man. Not because he was patient or noble, because he wasn't. He was going to do it because when she believed in her fire, she was going to be hell on wheels in bed. That's when she would throw herself at a man, teasing and driving him crazy with her hot hands and soft lips.

And he was going to be that man, too.

Tonight.

"Come here," he said softly. But instead of tugging Marcy closer, he turned her to face the window, standing behind her, his hands resting on her shoulders. With the light behind them, it was like looking into a mirror.

"*That's* beautiful," he told her, watching her eyes widen as he nudged the yellow fabric aside. It flowed like honey down her shoulders and arms, falling in a pool at their feet.

Nick wrapped an arm around her waist, splaying his fingers across her belly and pressing her back against him. When he cupped her breast with his other hand, touching the beaded tip with his thumb, Marcy gasped and closed her eyes.

"Nick!" It felt as if the lightning had moved inside her, a dazzling finger shooting from her nipple to the heated tension between her thighs.

"Can you feel what you do to me?" His breath fanned her ear. She opened her eyes and nodded just in time to watch him lower his arm so his hand cupped the triangle of auburn hair above her thighs. She shivered in anticipation and felt her nipples tighten almost painfully.

"Yes?" he murmured.

Marcy nodded, holding her breath. "Yes."

His finger touched the damp softness, and Marcy jolted back against him. *"Nick."*

"Does it hurt? Should I stop? Do you like it?" The questions came fast, a contrast to the gentle stroking.

"No! I don't know! *Yes!* Damn you, Nick Stoner," she panted, "you're driving me crazy. I'll get even, if it's the last thing I do."

His chuckle infuriated her. "I'm counting on it, sweet-heart."

Lightning flashed outside, erasing their images from the window. Marcy blinked and spun around, breathing as if she had run a marathon. She hooked her thumbs in the elasticized waistband of his sweats and pushed, kneeling down to finish the job. Nick stepped out of the pants and kicked them aside.

Still on her knees, Marcy looked up. Nick ignored the fact that he was naked and that he was blatantly, magnif-icently aroused. He just stood there, waiting. And he was beautiful.

She looked higher, at the expression on his face. It was a complicated blend of amused delight, expectation and anticipation. And a fierce hunger that threatened his mas-sive control.

It was exactly what she wanted to see. What she needed to see.

Nick Stoner made her feel, for the first time in her life, complete. Like a woman. A beautiful, wanton, *sexy* woman. A woman who could drive a man out of his mind, who could fulfill every one of his fantasies and add a few touches of her own.

Marcy smiled up at him and sat back on her heels. Touching her palms to the inside of his legs just above his knees, she murmured, "Payback time, Stoner. Are you ready?"

Something dark flickered in his eyes and he grinned. Marcy took that for a yes.

She worked her way up his thighs, taking her time, threading her fingers in the crisp, dark hair, kneading and smoothing the long muscles. When his hair became denser, she cupped her hands around him, cradling him in her palms.

"Does this feel good?" There was wonder in her voice.

"God, yes." All the amusement was gone. "Don't stop."

Marcy didn't. She explored the hard, glorious length of him, smiling when a tremor shot through him, touching the velvety tip with gentle fingers until he sucked in his breath.

"Enough." Nick's voice was strangled. He reached down, closing his hands around her wrists, thinking she looked like a treasure hunter who had just discovered a jewel-encrusted chest. And maybe she had, but she was going to kill him while she was examining the goodies.

"Don't stop me now," she protested with an exultant grin, intoxicated by his response. "I'm just getting started."

"Save it," he said briefly, tugging her to her feet. "For later."

"But—"

"Or there won't be a later."

He started to wrap his arms around her, but Marcy shook her head. Her eyes gleaming with determination, she spread her hands on his chest and gave a tentative shove, pushing him back toward the bed. Nick was more than willing.

When they reached it, she waited long enough for him to toss back the covers and pluck a foil-covered packet from the bedside table; then she threw herself in his arms. Nick fell back on the bed, taking her with him, rolling over until she was caged between him and the mattress.

His grin, Marcy decided, definitely belonged on a pirate. She poked a finger at his chest and said, "Uh-uh."

Nick stilled, gazing down at her, a sudden frown drawing his brows together. "No?"

She grinned. "I'm on a roll, Stoner, and I sure can't do anything down here."

Closing his eyes for a few seconds, Nick exhaled sharply. "Marcy," he began in a strained voice, "there are certain limits—"

"A *real* roll, Stoner," she said urgently. "Don't stop me now."

"I've created a monster." Nick groaned and rolled to his back.

Marcy propped herself up on her elbow and smoothed a hand over his chest. "You'll be proud of your creation one day," she predicted absently.

Nick gazed at her from narrowed eyes. He knew he would. If he lived that long. Hell, he was already. She hadn't just lost her initial uncertainty, she had jumped in headlong with all her habitual zest. Right now she looked like a kid at Christmas confronted with a pile of gifts, wondering which one to open first. Another tremor shot through him at the thought.

"Closer," Marcy muttered to herself, touching his belly with inquisitive fingers. "I need to be closer."

Nick solved her problem by scooping her up and settling her on top of him, balancing her until she gripped his hips with her knees. Bracing her hands on his chest, she looked down at him, luxuriating in his small, sexy smile and the glint of satisfaction in his dark eyes. Somewhere along the way, she realized complacently, they had stopped asking questions.

Leaning forward until her hair brushed his chest, Marcy forgot to tease. Intent on giving and receiving pleasure, she inched down, touching her lips to his. The kiss deepened, each of them giving, taking, touching, demanding. She shifted, giving him access to her breast. When he touched the tip with his tongue, Marcy gave a small, shaken cry.

Nick stopped. "What?"

Hardly hearing his husky question, she gasped, "I want you, Nick. I really want you. *Now!*"

"It's about time." His hands settled on her waist, tightened, prepared to lift her.

"No." She shook her head. "Right here." She sat up, her hands on his shoulders and said again, "Here. Now."

Nick reached down to the softness between her thighs and touched her, tenderly, deliberately, until she shuddered and grabbed his hand.

"Nick," she said urgently. "Now!"

He helped her ease down on him, gripping her thighs as small, convulsive shivers rippled through her, drawing him deeper into her warm sheathe.

"Nick?" Her eyes widened with shock and uncertainty.

"It's all yours, babe," he said exultantly. "Take it!"

She cried out, her knees tightening, her back arching. Waves of molten shudders lapped through her. And just as the heat, tension and unutterable pleasure exploded within her, Nick gave in to his own shattering climax.

Marcy collapsed on his chest, shivering with reaction. She was vaguely aware when he shifted her to his side and pulled the covers over them. She drifted near the edge of sleep, noting with drowsy interest the small aftershocks that lapped over her.

"Nick?" She nestled closer.

"Hmm?"

"I was going to make it last all night."

"We'll make up for it later."

She nodded, hearing the smile in his voice.

And they did. Twice during the night they reached for each other, teasing, soothing, exciting, touching, crying out in release.

Early the next morning Marcy opened her eyes, aware that something cataclysmic had taken place, wondering what it was. Looking around the room—Nick's room—gave her the first clue. His clothes were rumpled on the floor and next to them her robe looked like a puddle of sunlight.

Moving her legs gave her the second clue. She ached in a number of highly unlikely places.

Marcy blinked, grateful for the trick of nature that kept her from waking too suddenly. Greeting the morning light was always a shock to her system, and she had a feeling that this morning was going to be especially rough.

She gingerly turned her head, hoping against hope that she was wrong, that there was a logical explanation for her presence in Nick's bed, that he wasn't actually pressed up against her, taking up three-quarters of the mattress.

He was. On his stomach. Looking supremely content.

What's more, he was naked.

And even worse, so was she.

Coffee, she thought desperately, sliding to the edge of the bed. At this point caffeine was the only thing that could save her sanity. It might also clear her mind enough so she could remember exactly what had worked the transformation from kitten to wildcat.

She frowned and leaned closer to look at Nick's shoulders. Or more specifically the half-moon marks from her nails on his shoulders.

Oh, Lord. She closed her eyes, appalled, feeling heat flood her throat and cheeks. On second thought, she decided grimly, easing off the bed, it wasn't her memory that needed prodding. Apparently that was working only too well. She had a strong hunch that coffee wouldn't help the real problem.

What she needed was to have her head examined.

Having settled that to her satisfaction, Marcy scooped up her robe and fled to the kitchen.

Nick opened his eyes just in time to see Marcy's bare bottom disappear. Grinning, he rolled over and folded his hands behind his head.

Damn, he felt good.

He hadn't felt like this in months. Years. Gazing thoughtfully at the ceiling, he thought of her initial determined do-it-by-the-book seduction, and his smile faded. But Marcy O'Bannon of the Santa Barbara O'Bannons was a quick learner. In less time than he could count she had turned into a teasing wildcat.

And he had been the lucky man she had dug her claws into.

He grinned again. Hell, he had *never* felt this good.

He surged off the bed, whistling tunelessly, and headed for the shower. Letting the water beat down on him, he lined up the ducks as he saw them.

She needed some time alone.

It was understandable, he supposed. Last night she had met a Marcy O'Bannon she hadn't known existed. So she was going to have a double handful of reasons and excuses why they should go back to square one while she regrouped.

He could let her go or put her in a cage. Either way, he ran the risk of losing her. And he wasn't going to let that happen.

He shut off the water and reached for a towel, drying briskly. Looking into the steamy mirror, he blinked, seeing Marcy as she had been last night. If he lived to be three hundred, he would never forget the passion in her flushed cheeks and bright eyes, her hair sliding on his chest as if it had a life of its own, her exultant cries.

He wrapped the towel around his waist and stalked back into the bedroom, struck by a grim thought. Did she have the crazy idea that she could repeat what happened last night with another man?

Well, she could just damn well think again.

Eight

Plan *C*, Nick reminded himself, coming to a stop in the kitchen doorway.

C for compromise.

Since he couldn't let her run away and he wouldn't try to cage her, compromise was the only option left. And maybe it would give him time to figure out what the hell he was doing. More to the point, why he was feeling so outraged, so…possessive. Yeah, he admitted grimly, that was the word. Possessive. The last emotion he'd ever expected to feel, especially since he'd deliberately avoided women who thought in terms of permanency. That was a road that led to a world of grief. He didn't want any part of it, and he wasn't about to drop a load like that on Marcy's slim shoulders.

So what did he want? No strings, no obligations on either side? He shook his head, his eyes narrowing in irri-

tation. Hell, no. He wanted Marcy, now and tonight and...
He didn't know. He just wanted her.

Marcy stood with her back to him, staring out the window, clutching a mug of coffee between her hands. From the looks of the pot, she had already downed several cups.

She was edgy. It didn't take a cop or a psychic to figure that out. Marcy was standing still but from all the nervous energy zinging around the room, you'd swear she was pacing, drumming her fingers and tap-dancing all at the same time.

She was wearing yellow today. Her shorts were the walking kind, pleated and boxy, riding a few inches above her knees. The sleeveless shirt was loosely tucked in the band of her shorts. If it was an outfit designed to cool him down, it failed miserably. He had seen her last night without a stitch on, had traced every curve and hollow of her eager body, first with his hands and then his lips. She didn't have to wear tight clothes to make him hot and hard. He had been that way before he even opened his eyes. And if she knew what his imagination was doing with that prim little outfit, she'd run screaming out of the room.

Nick's grin faded when his gaze settled on the narrow band of fabric tied at her nape. He didn't like her hair pulled back and subdued. He wanted it as wild and free as it had been last night, silky and sliding through his fingers. He scowled, directing all of his banked hostility at the yellow scarf.

At least she wasn't running away.

The realization jerked him away from his contemplation of the knotted scarf. She was jittery and gulping down enough caffeine to keep her awake for the next three days, but she wasn't in her bedroom packing and she wasn't heading for her jazzy little car.

Plan C, he reminded himself, stepping into the kitchen.

"Good morning."

Marcy spun around at the sound of his voice and looked up just as Nick dropped a kiss on her parted lips. It was a deliberate kiss, fast and hard and possessive. While she was still getting her breath, he turned away to pour himself some coffee.

Holding her mug in front of her like a shield, Marcy scowled at his back. His bare back. All he had on was a pair of tan jeans, running shoes and—she gave a silent groan—several crescent-shaped indentations from her nails on his broad shoulders.

This wasn't going to be easy, she thought for the thousandth time. Staring out the window hadn't helped. Three cups of coffee hadn't inspired her. She still didn't know how to tell him that she was suffering from an acute case of the-morning-after-the-night-before, that she was in full retreat. How was she supposed to explain that to the man who had turned her into a sexual maniac just a few hours ago? A man who had every right to think he was hell on wheels in bed. A man who, damn it, *was* hell on wheels in bed.

The whole thing was crazy. And in the cold light of day, more than a bit embarrassing. Marcy closed her eyes, hoping he'd disappear, that it was all a nightmare. Marcy O'Bannon, Princess Humdrum of the Bedroom, couldn't have teased and touched him until they'd both gone up in flames. She couldn't have.

A moment's reflection assured her that she had.

Oh, God.

She opened her eyes to find Nick watching her, waiting with his patented water-dripping-on-rocks patience. Why did she do everything the hard way, she wondered miserably. Why couldn't she have fallen in love with the home-and-hearth type? Why did it have to be with a maverick, a semi-loner, a man who never mentioned the words love or commitment, who never talked of the future?

"I wish you wouldn't sneak up on me like that," she grumbled, swigging down another jolt of caffeine.

Nick grinned and came back to stand beside her. "The directions came in my supercop kit." He touched his mug to hers in a toasting gesture and took a swallow, watching her calmly over the rim. "Anything else bothering you this morning?"

"Now that you mention it, yes." Everything. "I...wish you wouldn't kiss me like that."

"How?" His innocent look wouldn't have fooled an infant. "You mean this way?" He cupped her chin with his hand and bent his head.

Marcy felt his breath, then his lips in just a whisper of a touch, tempting, tasting. His kiss deepened, demanded, his tongue touching hers. It seemed to last no more than a second, and forever.

He dropped his hand, and she backed away. "Yes," she said breathlessly. "Just like that."

"Why not?" He gave her a level look and took the battle to her court. "I did last night, and you didn't seem to mind." He grinned again. "In fact, as I remember it—"

"Yes! I'm sure you have an excellent memory," Marcy interrupted. Unfortunately, so did she, and that wasn't making this conversation a bit easier. After a pause that threatened to become uncomfortable, she added lamely, "Being a cop and all."

"Yeah. Cops are hell on wheels when it comes to remembering things."

Marcy jumped and darted a suspicious look at him. His expression was too bland to be true, she decided morosely. His dark eyes were the true indicators of his mood, and they told her in no uncertain terms that he was just aching for a fight.

"We have to talk," she said abruptly.

"It's about time."

Marcy turned on her heel and strode over to the bar. As she climbed on the end stool, she wondered if he had deliberately repeated the words he'd used the night before, when she had cried out that she wanted him.

Probably.

She didn't see Nick as the type to make things easy when he was being deprived of something he wanted. And he wanted her. Very much. At least, for now.

Those were the operative words. For now.

And that wasn't enough for her. She might be impulsive and rash, her motto for work might be *Have notebook, will travel,* but when it came to the important things like commitment, like...marriage, she wasn't a temporary person.

An affair, even with a man who had proved beyond a shadow of a doubt that she was all the woman she'd ever dreamed of being, wouldn't satisfy her or her need for stability. No, she had waited twenty-seven years and when she finally took the leap, she wanted the whole ball of wax—marriage and a family.

Nick slid onto the stool next to her, his shoulder and knee brushing against hers. "Is this where you tell me that last night didn't mean anything and ask me to be a gentleman and forget it? Because if it is," he said roughly, "I'll tell you right now, I'm no gentleman and I don't give up when I want something."

"Why doesn't that surprise me," she murmured, distantly noting that her knuckles were white from her death grip on the mug.

"No," Marcy said with an honesty that she knew would cost her dearly. "This is where I say that last night was...something I never expected to happen. It was—" she searched for the proper words and finally gave a wry smile ''—a real eye-opener.''

Darting an oblique glance at him, she added quietly, "And you were everything I ever hoped to find in a man." Her careless shrug was a work of art. She was determined to get through the next few moments without embarrassing either of them. "You were understanding, gentle and...sexy as all get-out. You gave me the gift of my own sexuality, femininity. Call it whatever you want, you gave it to me."

"Wrong, honey." Nick's voice was tight.

When he cleared his throat, Marcy shot him another glance, blinking at his profile, at a cheek that was slowly turning red. He was blushing, she thought in astonishment. Mr. Macho Cop was actually blushing!

"I didn't give you a damned thing but confidence." He took the mug out of her hands and set it on the counter before turning to face her; then he swung her around until her knees were trapped between his.

"You had the passion," he told her. "You've always had it. It shows in everything you do and it's been waiting to pour out. Hell, lady, last night in my arms you were hotter than the lightning bolts tearing up the sky."

Nick gave a short laugh at her look of astonishment. "Think about it," he urged. "I didn't hold a seminar last night. I didn't teach you a damn thing. I gave you the opportunity, and you reached out and took it in your hot, little hands."

"Nick!" Marcy groaned and covered her face. When she dropped her hands, she shot him a look that should have charred his shirt.

"Sorry." His grin was unrepentant. "That didn't come out the way I meant it." He waited, watching the emotions chase across her expressive face. "All right," he sighed, "what's the rest? I can see you're gearing up for something else."

Marcy felt as if she were walking across a mine field. Picking her words carefully, she began, "Even though last night was..."

"Beyond your wildest dreams?" Nick asked helpfully.

"Wonderful," Marcy said primly. "I have to admit that it..."

"Scared the living hell out of you."

"That's putting it a little stronger than I would have," Marcy said thoughtfully, blinking in surprise at his evaluation. Was he right? she wondered. If he was, it was at her own loss of control rather than his uninhibited appreciation of her body.

"And I suppose what you're trying to say is that you need time to..." He shrugged. "Adjust." Plan C, he reminded himself.

Marcy felt the tension between them mount when he hesitated before finally selecting the innocuous word. It jumped several notches while he waited for her reply. It wasn't exactly what she had in mind, but she was flexible, she thought cravenly. Time would work just fine, especially if it lasted until she finished the article and took off on the next leg of the assignment, or until he went back to work. Which ever came first.

"Yes," she said firmly, deciding to push as far as she could while he seemed in the mood to negotiate. "That's exactly what I was going to say. But that's only part of it. I want your promise that you're not going to pressure me."

Nick's eyes narrowed. "You don't want much, do you?"

"Of course," she added, not even blinking, "we could make it easy on both of us. One of us could leave."

"All right," he said abruptly. "You need time? You got it. Beyond that, no promises. I'll tell you again that you're as safe with me as you want to be. I'm not going to drag you, kicking and screaming, to bed. But that doesn't mean I'll let you forget what we had last night. Or that we could have it again any time you're willing to trust."

Marcy scowled. "Trust who? You?"

"No." Nick shook his head. "You already do. You proved that last night in my arms. Think about it." He dropped a swift, teasing kiss on the tip of her nose. "Now, what do you want for breakfast?"

"Nick, listen to this." Marcy fingered the feather she had picked up at the Mulroony mansion and waited for him to look up from his book of crossword puzzles. It had been forty-eight hours since their discussion, and he had been on relatively good behavior. That is, if several kisses that had been as shattering as they were light, glances that didn't even try to conceal their hunger, and periods of unbearable tension could be called good behavior. For Nick Stoner, it probably was.

Forty-eight hours of lectures, given by Marcy O'Bannon *to* Marcy O'Bannon, the thrust of which was that Nick Stoner was a whole lot of trouble, a barrelful of grief. So why wasn't she listening?

Because she was crazy. Because she was crazy about *him*. Because he had touched her heart—okay, and her body—the way no other man ever had. Because—

"More research?" He tilted his head, indicating the pile of books scattered around her.

"Always. I have a fount of trivia at my fingertips," she assured him. "For instance, do you know where the word *Mojave* came from?"

"I give."

"Probably from a native word *hamakhave*. It means 'three mountains' and refers to some sharp, pointed peaks near Needles, California."

He grinned, enjoying her enthusiasm. Passion. Right now, he'd take it however he could get it.

"But this is what I wanted to tell you." She ran a slim finger down a page, muttering. "Oh, here it is. They liked to use bird feathers for ornaments. They put them on bracelets, headpieces and wands. And they often put split feathers on the ends of their arrows." She waggled her hand, drawing his attention to the feather she held.

Nick groaned. "Are you heading where I think you're heading with this?"

"Don't be so obstinate. Each time Zelda heard the cry she found one, and the same thing happened to me. At least admit it's possible. The feather *could* be a message."

He shook his head. "No way."

"Okay, if you don't buy the message theory, do you have a better one?"

"Yeah. Joshua Junction has molting birds. Lots of them."

"That's pretty weak, Stoner. Can't you do any better than that."

He scowled. "No, I can't. My way isn't working any better than yours."

"What do you mean, 'your way?'"

"I called Jackson the night of the storm and asked him to check out the place. He got back to me this morning."

"Your partner?" When he nodded, she said on a rising note, "The Mulroony house?"

"Yeah."

"Nick, so help me God, if you bring the law down on us, I'll—"

"It's already down on you," he interrupted. "*I'm* the law, remember."

"You're on sick leave. Besides, I'm talking about the ones tromping around, ruining vibes and bringing reporters in their wake."

"Vibes," he muttered in disgust. "Give me a break."

"What did he say?"

Nick blinked. "Who?"

"Jackson, your other half."

"Nothing. No one's interested in the place. Not the drug boys, not Immigration. It's as clean as a whistle."

"Aha!" Marcy grinned. "So what does that leave?"

"Questions, not ghosts."

"Stoner, you have a one-track mind." Marcy carefully set the book aside and crossed her legs tailor fashion, wanting to laugh out loud at his wary expression. For some reason she couldn't fathom, she loved arguing with this stubborn, narrow-minded pragmatist.

"Will you give me this much?" She held her index finger and thumb about an inch apart. "Will you admit that there are some things that simply can't be explained in a logical or rational manner?"

"Like Zelda's mind?"

"I was thinking more along the lines of ESP and precognition."

"Oh, that." He dismissed it with a wave of his large hand.

"Yes, that. Come on, Stoner, you're a cop, and I'm assuming that you're a good one. Haven't you ever been on a case and had a warning come out of nowhere? A little voice that told you something was wrong?"

He stared at her, his face expressionless.

"Ha!" She gave him a triumphant grin. "I knew it. You have! Okay, Stoner, here's the sixty-four-thousand dollar question. Answer it right and you win the prize. What do you call it?"

"A little voice," he said dryly.

Marcy groaned. "You would. But I have to tell you, Sherlock, that some people call it instinct. Others would call it highly developed instinct. And a few enlightened souls would refer to it as ESP. Now are you going to tell me that you've never heard of a police department bringing in a psychic to work on a case with them?"

"I have."

The two short words told her exactly what he thought of the situation. "And some of them got results, didn't they?" she persisted.

Nick muttered something about luck.

Marcy shook her head. "I don't think so."

"I checked out a lot of phony psychics when I worked in bunco," he said in exasperation. "They were nothing but people on the take, frauds."

"It's possible," Marcy agreed, nodding. "It's a field that brings out all the fruitcakes and charlatans. You investigated the ones people complained about, so the odds are that they were phonies. But I've looked into the subject, too, for a series I did on extrasensory perception. The only difference was, I was investigating the people reputed to be genuine."

He nodded. "I read the articles."

"Then you know that I believe they exist, people with a highly developed sixth sense."

Nick groaned. "What are we talking about here? Ghosts or psychics? And what does one have to do with the other?"

Marcy's smile faded. "I guess what I'm wondering is, if one exists—and I've already said I believe there are some genuine psychics—is it possible that the other does, too?"

Nick stared at her, almost speechless. But not quite. "Like a dead Indian who screams like a banshee? Come on, Marcy, you can do better than that."

"You're supposed to keep an open mind about this."

"I'm the skeptic, remember?"

"Yoo-hoo!" Zelda's exuberant trill burbled through the front screen door.

"Speaking of fruitcakes," Nick sighed. "We haven't seen this one in a few days. You know, there are times when I look forward to going back to simple things like—"

"Murder and mayhem?"

He thought about it for a second. "Yeah. Doesn't sound bad at all."

"Marcy? Nick? Where are you?" Zelda opened the door and poked in her head. "There you are!" She breezed in and dropped down on the couch near Marcy. "You'll never guess what I've been doing!" Her curls bobbed and her brown eyes sparkled with excitement.

Nick held up his hand to stop her. "Don't tell me. Let me guess." He thought a second and then, sounding like a man who had stretched his imagination to the limit, said, "You've had a breakthrough with your crystal ball and you're ready to hold a séance."

Zelda's face fell. "You knew! I've been sequestered for three days, studying." She turned to Marcy. "Men are so logical. But I suppose it shouldn't have surprised me with Nick. The dear boy is used to dealing with facts and arriving at the proper conclusion."

Nick choked. "Facts? You show me one hard fact in this craziness and I'll—"

"Or—" Zelda swung back to face him, her eyes even brighter "—are you developing . . . other areas?"

"No." Nick's voice was harassed. "I am not."

"Logic is all well and good, but our lives are much richer when we incorporate *all* of our senses. And we all have the ability to tune in, so to speak. Why, just the other night, Gray Feather was telling me that you would make an excellent medium. Because of your instincts, you know. He said you should never ignore them."

"Exactly what I was just telling Nick," Marcy agreed, grinning at him. "His instincts were working overtime the night of the storm," she explained hastily when Zelda turned curious eyes on her. "I was out in it, and he was worried about me."

"Very commendable," Zelda said with an approving nod at Nick, "but quite unnecessary. I taught her how to protect herself."

Nick sighed. "I suppose you have a black belt in karate."

Making a sound that sounded like *tch,* Zelda shook her head. "Violence is also quite unnecessary."

"I'm going to hate myself for asking," Nick muttered, gazing at Marcy. Her face had gone suspiciously blank. "What's the secret weapon? One of Gray Feather's tricks, I suppose."

She hesitated. "I don't know if you're ready for this. It's pretty sophisticated stuff."

"Don't push it, O'Bannon."

"I close my eyes and picture myself surrounded by a white light."

"I knew I shouldn't ask."

"Then I say, 'I am safe wherever I am.'"

"That's it?" Nick said mildly.

She nodded, a small smile lifting the corners of her mouth.

"That's *it?*"

She nodded again.

"You need a keeper, lady." His glare included Zelda. "You both do. There are muggers and killers, rapists and drug crazies out there, and you two turn on a mental light bulb and tell yourself you're safe? I don't believe it."

Zelda reached over and patted his knee. "Someday it will all make sense."

"Don't count on it," Nick said, swinging to his feet. "I need a beer. Can I get something for you?"

"No, thanks," the women murmured together.

"Marcy!" Zelda hissed as soon as he was out of sight. "I saw something!"

"Where?" Marcy looked over her shoulder.

"In the crystal ball!" Her announcement was made in a thrilled whisper that set her curls jiggling behind her beaded headband. "I saw it clear as day!"

"Good heavens. What was it?"

"Oh, well, I'm not sure."

Marcy frowned. "What do you mean, you're not sure? How can you tell that you saw something, if you don't know what it was?"

"I *know* I did," Zelda said stubbornly. "Even Nick sensed it as soon as I walked in the door. He knew I had a breakthrough. I *saw* something, Marcy! And you know what that means. Now we can have a séance!"

Marcy's frown deepened. "I don't know, Zelda. It seems to me we should at least wait until you can make out what you're seeing."

"It was big," the older woman offered. "Very big." She brightened. "I think it was the Mulroony house. I think we're supposed to go there."

"And *I* think you're clutching at straws," Marcy said dryly. "You just want to creep over there in the dead of night and put on a show."

Zelda drew herself up. "I resent that. And so does Gray Feather." She considered the accusation for a minute, then grinned. "It wouldn't be a show, it would be a spectacular! Gray Feather does nothing in half measures. Come on, Marcy, let's do it!"

Marcy looked at the older woman, felt her excitement. "Why not?" she said slowly. "It's safe enough. At least the strong arm of the law considers it so." She explained that Nick's partner had run a check on the house.

"You mean Nick thought *drugs* were being sold there?" Zelda sounded thrilled.

"He's a cop, remember? He's paid to think like that."

"But what about the screams? They're real. I know I heard them."

"I did, too. The night of the storm." Marcy looked thoughtful. "I wonder if there's a comedian in the area. Someone who likes to play practical jokes and rigged up a tape?"

"We can look when we go over there," Zelda tempted. "And if we can't find it that way, maybe we'll discover something during the séance." A doubtful expression crossed her face. "Should we invite Nick?"

"If you want a séance, I advise you to forget the dear boy," Marcy said dryly. "He'd lock us in our rooms if he even got a hint of it. *After* he told us the idea was crazy, we were crazy for even thinking of it, that the house would fall in around our ears, and while there was no actual proof that something illegal, immoral, dangerous or fattening was going on over there, he—"

"Oh, dear. Hush! Here he comes!"

Nick stood in the doorway and took a long swallow of the cold beer. "I've been thinking."

Zelda looked up. "Yes, Nick?"

"You're not actually considering having a séance, are you? Especially at that wreck of a house?"

"Why do you ask?" Zelda's eyes were round with innocence.

"Because that's all you've talked about for this last week," he retorted, going back to his chair and collapsing in it. "The idea is crazy, and so are you if you're still thinking about it. I had the place checked out—"

"Marcy told me." Zelda smiled at him. "That was thoughtful of you."

His brows drew together in a frown. "It wasn't thoughtful, it was logical. Even if the place is just what it seems to be—"

"A sad, lonely, deserted house," Zelda inserted helpfully.

"—it's still dangerous. The floors are probably rotted, the wall could cave in—"

"That's exactly what Marcy was just saying," Zelda told him, stopping him in his tracks.

"She was?"

"Almost word for word."

"I'm glad somebody's finally showing some sense," he muttered.

"Oh, well." Zelda gave a mournful sigh. "I *did* want to do it, but if it's dangerous..." Her voice dwindled away. "Maybe some afternoon we'll do it at my house," she added with a brave little smile.

A sudden yawn overtook her. "'Scuse me." She patted her mouth with her fingers. "I was up late last night, studying. I think I'll go take a little nap."

She rested her hand on Nick's shoulder in a fleeting gesture of farewell. Turning to Marcy, she waggled her brows meaningfully. "Call me sometime," she said casually. "Bye, dear."

Nick eyed her with deep suspicion as she drifted out the door. "I don't like it."

"Don't like what?" Marcy murmured, picking up her book and opening it to the page she had marked.

"She caved in too quick. Behind that wide-eyed expression, she's cooking something up."

Marcy grinned. "Sherlock, for once I agree with you. I think she's plotting dark plots. I also think that, knowing your suspicious nature, she's trying to lull you into a false sense of security, hoping you'll think she's given up the idea. I wouldn't be surprised if she's going back to her place to brood and try to outsmart you. She'll come back in a few days with a whole new plan, ready to start the attack all over again."

Nick prowled around the room, stopping at the bookshelves built into one wall. His fingers skimmed the titles as he glanced over at Marcy. She was still sitting on the floor reading, doing it as she did everything—with passion. And taking notes. With even more passion.

Warmth poured through the window along with an arrow of light that turned her hair to bright fire. Propping one shoulder against the wall, he wondered how long it would be before he cracked. He tried to picture her reaction, if he snatched her up and buried his face in that glorious hair.

She'd think he was crazy.

His plan wasn't the stroke of brilliance it had seemed two days ago, he admitted, watching Marcy absently brush her hair away from her face. It had backfired with a vengeance, mainly because it had given him time to think.

Too much time.

He had never felt possessive about a woman. Never. Until now. Their isolation at Cristobel's house was just fine with him because he didn't want another man watching Marcy traipse around in her shorts. Hell, he thought in disgust, he was even jealous of the old geezers in town who looked as much as they talked when she interviewed them.

And he never thought of a woman in terms of commitment. Until now. He wanted Marcy tied to him with all the strings and trappings. Not just until he went back to San Diego or she finished her article. He wanted her for a lifetime, for...ever.

But Marcy was a creature of sunlight, and he had spent too much time in the shadows. He moved over to the window, looking out in the direction of the Mulroony place. Its chances of rejuvenation were about the same as his spending the rest of his life with Marcy, he reflected, jamming his hands in his back pockets. Zip. The statistics for cops were bleak—both in terms of divorce and life expectancy.

He was the realist in the crowd, he reminded himself. He couldn't dodge either the statistics or the fact that he was a cop, had been for ten years and would stay one for as long as his luck lasted. Loving Marcy had nothing to do with it. Being a cop was as much his identity as his name.

And he had no right to drag Marcy into a life like that. He had seen too many women wither and change from the stress. Their lives were spent waiting for disaster, wondering when it would come. Not if it would, but when.

He wouldn't do that to her. He—

"Nick?" Marcy's voice was soft. "What's the matter? You're as restless as a cat before a storm. Come here." She patted the floor beside her.

Nick turned from the window, gazing down at her. She looked like an anxious sprite frowning up at him. A generous sprite who would take care of others before she thought of saving her own skin. He stayed where he was, knowing if he went over there, Plan *C*, pathetic as it was, would be shot to hell. There was no way he could keep his hands off her.

She held out a hand and smiled up at him. "Come on, sit down."

He walked over and took her hand, but instead of dropping down beside her, he tugged, bringing her to her feet.

"Nick! What are you doing?" Her fingers dug into his shoulders. Her green eyes were wide with surprise and dawning excitement.

"What I've been wanting to do for the last two days," he said, in a voice level with rigid control. "Make love to you. I've talked to myself for forty-eight hours and it hasn't done a bit of good, so if you want me to stop, say so right now, honey."

"I can't."

Nick exhaled sharply.

"Stop you, I mean. My lectures haven't done any good, either," she admitted reluctantly, sliding her hands around his neck.

Nick scooped her up. "I hope you mean it," he muttered, heading down the hall. "No regrets later?"

"No regrets," she promised, tracing his cheek with her fingertips. "None at all."

He kicked the bedroom door shut behind him. "Lock it," he said, holding her close enough to reach the knob.

At her questioning look, he said, "I don't want Zelda rushing in with the latest news from the great beyond."

Marcy locked it.

He set her down and reached for her shirt. Marcy shook her head and took a step back. "I'm in a hurry," she confessed with an honesty that took his breath away.

Seconds later their clothes were scattered around them and he picked her up, one arm beneath her knees, one across her back. Holding her against him, Nick took a deep breath, wondering how the magic of Marcy had happened to him—and how long it would last. He tightened his arms in a convulsive hug, then tossed her gently on the bed. For a long moment he stood gazing down at her wildfire hair spread over his pillow, at the languorous invitation in her green eyes. When she rolled on her side to face him, her breasts swaying gently with the movement, he forgot to breathe.

Color seeped into her cheeks and he knew he was embarrassing her, but she made no attempt to reach for the sheet to cover herself. Instead, she gave him a smile that almost brought him to his knees. Shifting restlessly, one long leg slightly bent at the knee, she waited, looking at him with frank appreciation. Her gaze dropped to his shoulders, traveled slowly down his chest, followed the narrow line of dark hair down his belly, lowered another notch and stopped.

When she blinked, he said in a tight voice, "That's what you do to me."

Marcy's smile was small and very feminine. "I know. And you can't imagine what that does to *me*."

He grinned at the purr of satisfaction in her voice, thinking with one part of his mind that patience was indeed its own reward. Marcy was no longer wary of her reaction to him, she had found her fire and reveled in it.

Eagerness shimmered in her brilliant green eyes, and his smile faded as quickly as it had come. Her sensual impatience was as arousing as the hollows and surprisingly lush curves of her small body.

When she smiled up at him in invitation, Nick's blood sang and he dropped down beside her, pulling her against him. "Ah, Marcy," he said against her lips, "I have to love you."

She ran her hand down his lean buttock and thigh, smiling at his response, murmuring huskily, "It's about time." Anticipation gleamed in her eyes as his head lowered. Her lips parted as his mouth covered hers and she moaned, pressing against him, holding him close as his lips traced a hot, moist path down the frantically beating pulse in her throat to the tip of her breast.

"Mmmm."

Nick grinned again at the sigh of sheer contentment, wondering if she had any idea how exciting that soft sound was.

"I changed my mind," Marcy said languidly.

He dropped a kiss on the tip of her nose. "How so?"

"I'm not in a hurry, after all." She prodded his shoulder with a slim finger until he rolled onto his back, then propped herself up on one elbow and smiled down at him. "I've been thinking."

Nick slid his fingers through her tumbled hair, framing the back of her head with his hand. "Umm?"

Smiling at the lazy question, Marcy asked one of her own. "Would you say I have a good imagination?"

Turning his head to kiss the tip of her breast, he muttered absently, "Top-notch."

"You're right." She trailed her fingers down the crisp hair on his chest. "And I've spent the last two days imagining this."

Nick stilled, his heart pounding beneath her hand. "This?" he asked thickly.

Marcy nodded. "This." She slid over and settled on top of him, her elbows resting on his shoulders, her chin cupped in her hands as she gazed down at him. Her expression was a blend of curiosity, eagerness and daring, and Nick's reaction caught him by surprise. Marcy wanted him as much as he wanted her. She wanted every square inch of him. Her teasing smile told him that she intended to drive him out of his mind, and she probably would. But there was just one small thing she hadn't considered. As soon as she sprang her sensual little trap, she would be caught in it right along with him.

His heart swelled with tenderness and his body tightened painfully with fierce excitement. He caught his breath when she shifted her slim legs until they rested on his, her toes brushing his shins, groaning when her soft body melted into his.

Marcy pressed a lingering kiss on his mouth, touching him delicately with the tip of her tongue. "Don't go away," she murmured, easing down to skim her lips over the curve of muscle on his chest.

As if he would.

As if he *could.*

Nick stiffened, listening to the blood roar through his veins, his hands tightening on her waist. She was going to drive him crazy.

And she knew exactly how to do it.

Marcy slid off of him, slowly, carefully rolling to his side. She sat up and looked. At him. Her soft eyes caressed every square inch, every curve of muscle, every hard plane, every dusting of crisp black hair. She began at his shoulders, made little forays across his chest, inspecting the flat nubs of flesh amid a scattering of dark hair, following the narrow, dusky trail down his hard abdomen.

Nick stopped breathing when she stilled, her gaze lingering on the thick gathering of black hair that did nothing to conceal his arousal. Years later, she blinked and moved downward, her eyes stroking his muscular thighs and long legs.

With nerve-shattering slowness, she reversed the process, working back up his body. When her gaze finally met his, Nick exhaled with a painful gasp. He didn't have the vaguest idea how long he had been holding his breath.

But Marcy wasn't through.

She touched his shoulder with her hand, sliding a finger over his smooth flesh down to a patch of crisp, springy hair. Across his ribs and diagonally up to the narrow, dusky band that arrowed downward. Nick gritted his teeth, waiting for the touch that just might cause an explosion that would end the torture sooner than she planned.

When it came, he thought he would go up in flames. But he didn't. He lived through it, shuddering when she brushed his ankle and began the upward journey, bucking when her fingers trailed up, over and around him. When her warm hand finally settled on his shoulder, Nick held it with his.

"Marcy—"

She shook her head, smiling, and leaned toward him, touching her lips to his throat.

"No more," he said hoarsely, but he would have died before he tried to stop her.

Her reply was a kiss that slid across his chest and the touch of her tongue on his hard nipple.

"My God, Marcy—"

Following the path that was sensitive to the point of pain, Marcy spread warm, moist kisses down his body. Her long hair brushed over him like a silky, fiery blanket. Perspiration beaded on Nick's brow. He needed her touch as a parched man needed water, though he might explode if he got it. Maybe die.

When it came, he didn't die.

"Marcy! Yes . . . oh, sweetheart. *Yes.*"

With an inarticulate cry, Nick grabbed Marcy by the shoulders and hauled her up beside him, settling her on her back. She slid her arms around his neck, welcoming him. When he eased his weight on her, her long legs wrapped around his hips, locking, holding him close as he entered her, her exultant cry of pleasure joining his.

Nine

Marcy opened her eyes, blinking in the darkness. She was nestled spoon fashion against Nick, her bare bottom tucked against his hard thighs. And she was smiling. It wasn't just a polite curve of her lips, she reflected, snuggling closer. It was a small, sensual, very female, I've-got-the-world-by-the-tail smile.

She brushed her toes down Nick's leg and his arm tightened around her waist. Her eyes narrowed, catlike, in satisfaction and her smile deepened.

Nick's hand was cupping her breast, and when his thumb touched her nipple in a gentle, rasping stroke, she sighed and settled more deeply against him, thinking of the past few hours. More than a few, she amended with another contented smile. Much more.

They had spent the afternoon making love. Hot, frantic, almost desperate love. If she had had any remaining doubts, if she had been worried that their first time had been a fluke—and of course she hadn't, she told herself bracingly—they had been eradicated. Nick was a deeply sensual man, a passionate man, a thoroughly uninhibited, passionate man. And he brought out the exact same qualities in her, she reflected with deep satisfaction.

After a shower, some good wine and a leisurely meal, they had returned to the bedroom, where Nick, with her full cooperation, again served and protected her. And later, yet again.

She ran her hand down his arm, tracing the pattern of crisp hair with her fingertips, her thoughts straying, wondering how they would blend the here and now with the future. How they would reconcile her rambling profession with his. If Nick would be able to wrap his tongue around the *C* word.

Commitment.

Somehow, she vowed, things would work out. Sooner or later.

She looked at the clock again and blinked. Time was passing. Too fast. Cristobel would be back in a day or so, Nick would return to work, she would have her article done soon and Zelda—

Good grief.

She stiffened, and Nick's arm tightened around her. Zelda was probably expecting her to call, waiting to pounce on the phone as soon as it rang. Her scatty friend had probably collected all of her paraphernalia and was ready to trundle up hill and down dale to a séance.

Marcy's eyes widened and she seriously considered the matter. Well, why not? Nick was enjoying the sleep of a sexy, exhausted man, and she was curious. She had never been to a séance. And even though Zelda was going to be in charge, she might learn something. And time, she reminded herself, was only one aspect of the intriguing situation. She might never again have the opportunity.

So why not?

When she couldn't come up with even one good reason, she half turned and dropped a kiss on Nick's shoulder. He murmured and ran his hand down her thigh. Later, my love, she promised silently.

Smiling, she eased out of the circle of his arms and slid to the side of the bed. Seconds later she unlocked the door and padded down the hall to her room.

Once she had on her jeans and shoes, Marcy rummaged through her closet. Since Nick had ruined her one dark sweatshirt, she settled for a pale yellow. Hardly a night-stalking outfit, but then there was no one or no thing out there to stalk, she reminded herself. At the last minute she grabbed a small backpack and headed for the door.

Zelda's house was awash with light when Marcy got there. She rang the bell, waited, and rang again. Finally, she turned the knob, found it open and walked in. She tracked down the older woman in the dining room.

"Ah, Marcy, there you are." Zelda looked up with a distracted smile. "I'm almost ready." Her only concession to the hike ahead of them was the tennis shoes on her small feet. Her dress drifted and swirled and a dozen bracelets jingled on her arm as she trotted around the room, selecting items and placing them on the table.

"How did you know I'd be here?" Marcy asked, eyeing the growing pile with both fascination and alarm. "I didn't call."

"I knew you'd come," Zelda said serenely, adding a flashlight to the collection.

Marcy decided she didn't want to know the source of her friend's knowledge. A scatty, entertaining Zelda with questionable ESP was one thing, but dealing with a genuine psychic was a whole different ball game. Nope, she told herself, wandering over to the table, she wasn't asking any questions if she couldn't deal with the answers.

"Are you sure we need all this stuff?" she asked in dismay. "It's not as if we have a mule, you know."

"Everything," Zelda said firmly.

Marcy opened her backpack. "Both of these?" She pointed to two branched candlesticks, each with three candles.

"Atmosphere," Zelda said with a nod. On a more practical note, she added, "It's the only light we'll have. There's no electricity, remember."

"Right." Marcy stuffed them in the bag. She added the flashlight, matches, a lace tablecloth, a knife and a hammer. "A hammer?" She wouldn't ask about the knife, she decided.

"In case the paneling sticks."

"What are these?" Marcy pointed to two squarish green things that vaguely resembled balloons.

"Inflatable cushions. We don't know how long we'll be there and the chairs are pretty hard." Zelda placed a translucent sphere on the table, wrapped it carefully in a soft cloth and put it in a box, while Marcy swept the remaining items into the pack.

"You really do have a crystal ball!" Marcy stared at the wrapped package uneasily.

"I told you I did."

"I know, but..." But she hadn't taken the older woman seriously, she realized. Somehow the whole idea of someone peering into a round glass stone had seemed like a joke. But now, trekking out to a deserted barn of a house on a dark night with a genuine—and obviously expensive—crystal ball didn't seem so funny.

"If you can manage that stuff, I'll carry this." Zelda slipped her burden into a straw shoulder bag and looked around. "Ready?" Her voice lifted with excitement.

"Ready," Marcy said feebly.

As they stepped out onto the porch, Zelda looked over at Cristobel's house. "Where's Nick?" she whispered.

"Asleep, and we'd better hope he stays that way." Marcy pulled the strap taut on the backpack.

"It would have been nice to have the dear boy along," Zelda said wistfully. "Three makes such a nice, cozy group."

"Be grateful for small blessings. We wouldn't have a group at all if he was here."

"No. He doesn't understand, does he?" Zelda sighed. "What a pity."

"Actually, I'm not sure that I do, either," Marcy admitted, starting down the stairs. "You *do* understand that I'm here because I'm curious, don't you? And not because I'm a firm believer in—"

"You have an open mind. That's enough." Zelda took off at a brisk pace. "Let's hurry. I can't wait to get started."

"Are you nervous?" Marcy asked after they had walked awhile in silence. Zelda was spry for her age, so they kept moving at a fair pace.

"Nervous?" When the older woman shook her head, her tight curls shook and glistened in the moonlight. "What's to be nervous about? Nick said the police couldn't find anything wrong, so that takes care of any earthly problems. And if spirits *are* there, they'll be friendly. Besides, we have our—"

"I know, white lights," Marcy said in resignation. Nick was right, she reflected uneasily. They sounded like a pretty pathetic defense if there were a problem, even coupled with

Zelda's safety mantra or affirmation or whatever she called it.

Stepping carefully in the rutted path, Marcy brooded about options. As she had told Nick repeatedly, she didn't expect trouble—earthly or spiritual, but if it came and she had a choice, she'd rather have Nick's gun. Not that she had even seen it or would know what to do with it if she *did* have it, but it packed a more lethal threat than a beam of light, she told herself as they puffed up one side of the hill and slid down the other.

"There it is," Zelda panted. "Isn't it beautiful? Come on!"

"How are we going to get in?" Marcy asked as they approached the house. "Those windows are too high and the ones in the basement are stuck."

"The back door," Zelda said over her shoulder, trotting around the corner of the house.

"You mean it's open?"

"Who would lock a deserted house in the middle of nowhere?"

"You have a point."

"Careful." Zelda skirted the center of the wooden porch. "That part's full of termites. Ah." There was a wealth of satisfaction in her voice when the door eased open. The two of them stepped inside. "Well, here we are," she said breathlessly. "What do you think?"

"I think that if Nick was right about termites in the porch, he might be right about the structure itself," Marcy said, glancing uneasily around the dark room.

"A hundred years ago they built things to last," Zelda said blithely. "And the dry air helps. Come on, let's go!"

Marcy grabbed a handful of gauzy dress. "Not so fast. Don't take a step until I get the flashlight," she ordered. "I don't want either of us falling through the floor." While

Zelda murmured about white lights and guardian spirits, Marcy shrugged out of the pack and opened the flap. "Here it is. Hold on just a minute."

She played the light over the floor. "Well," she said dubiously, "I don't see any holes. I suppose it's okay. Which way?"

Zelda trotted toward the opposite wall. "This was the parlor where they had their fanciest furniture and entertained company. It was the closest room to the front door, so everyone who came to call would have to walk through it and be properly impressed." As they passed through a doorway, she waved a hand in a circular motion, saying, "The living room, where the family gathered."

Marcy followed more slowly, testing the flooring, making wide, sweeping arcs with the flashlight and brushing aside several long, hanging cobwebs. "You seem to know a lot about the place," she commented when she reached the open door, trying not to think about the spiders that had produced the fragile snares and were undoubtedly lurking in the vicinity.

"I ran across a brochure about the house at the historical society. Complete with a floor plan." Zelda's voice drifted back to her, sounding hollow in the empty room. "That's where I got the idea of looking for a secret room off the dining area. The measurements didn't seem right," she added vaguely. "Ah! Here we are. The dining room. You'll have to come back during the day sometime to see the wainscoting."

Marcy absently flashed the light over the dark wood covering the lower three feet of the wall. "Good grief, look at the intricate carving! I'm surprised looters haven't come in and ripped it off."

"Umm." Zelda sounded preoccupied. "Bring the light over here. The little button's somewhere in this part."

Walking over to stand beside her, Marcy played the light over the area Zelda was fingering. "It's right around here. I know it is. I haven't been here in a while," she mumbled in apology.

"I'm surprised you found it at all." Marcy took another look around. "The room's enormous. How *did* you find it?"

"I was nosy, bored, stubborn and had a lot of time on my hands," Zelda said succinctly. "Ah! Here it is. See how this little knob fits right into the carved groove? You just move it to one side and push." As she followed her own directions, there was a soft snick and a narrow panel swung open.

Marcy divided her attention between the snazzy little door and the fingers turning the knob. One was as fascinating as the other. It had taken a master craftsman to create the hidden opening, but the woman who had located it was equally formidable.

There was an agile brain beneath those platinum curls, Marcy realized with a start. It was not by mere speculation or luck that Zelda had found the room. She had studied the architect's plans and calculated the square footage, then creatively and tenaciously set about proving her own theory.

So why was a woman with a brain like that playing the role of a frivolous psychic? Marcy stared down at her, unable to think of one good reason. Or was she playing? Could she be both brilliant *and* rattlebrained? An eccentric genius? Feeling a bit like Alice holding a tiger by the tail, she followed Zelda through the opening.

It was like walking into a cave.

Marcy stopped inside the door, beaming the light around the small room. It was only large enough to hold three or four people comfortably, she estimated, as the light skimmed over a fireplace and mantel, a small table and several wooden chairs. If some unfortunate soul had occupied the room for any length of time, he or she had done it in spartan surroundings.

"There!" Zelda brushed her dusty hands together. "Put the candelabras on the mantel and let's get some light in here." As Marcy obediently tended to that chore, lighting the long white tapers one by one and filling the room with a golden glow, Zelda bustled around domestically, blowing a cloud of dust off the table and covering it with the lace cloth. "There!" she said again. "Gray Feather likes pretty things."

A quick look at the chairs told Marcy all she needed to know. They were as dusty as the table. Grateful for Zelda's practical streak, she inflated the pads and dropped them on the seats. She eased down on one to watch Zelda unveil the star of the show.

First, Zelda unwrapped a brass pedestal and placed it on the table, moving it several times until she found the perfect spot. Next came the crystal ball, buffed until her fingerprints were removed and gently deposited on the stand. She stood back, tilted her head and finally nodded approvingly. "There!" she said a third time.

"Sit down," she told Marcy, waving her to a seat.

Intrigued, Marcy sat. The glass ball reflected the lights from the candles until it seemed to glow with an inner light of its own. "Am I supposed to do anything?" she asked uncertainly.

"Think calm thoughts," Zelda murmured, concentrating on the crystal.

Glancing over her shoulder at the open panel, she asked, "Should I close the door before we get started?"

Zelda shook her head, sending her curls bobbing. "It might take us a while to get out. I never bothered looking for the lever on this side."

Half asleep, Nick turned over, automatically reaching for Marcy. When his hand slid across the mattress, he jolted awake, adrenaline pumping through his body. The sheet was still warm, one part of his mind registered. She was probably in the bathroom or getting a drink of water. Another part reminded him that she had a penchant for disappearing in the middle of the night, and when she went she usually ended up at an old house over a mile away.

He flung back the covers and grabbed his clothes. If he found her in the kitchen, he could always tell her he was restless and couldn't sleep. It wasn't terrific, but it would do in a pinch. If she wasn't there, at least this time he'd be dressed.

He was zipping his pants and stepping into his shoes when the phone rang. Tension kicked in, knotting the muscles in his belly. Nick closed his eyes and swore. No one called at one in the morning with good news. No one.

He caught it on the second ring, knowing who it was before he picked it up. He had been expecting it, unconsciously waiting for it. "Yeah?"

"You awake, partner?"

"Yeah, Jackson, I'm here."

"About that house you wanted checked?"

He rubbed the back of his neck, working the jangled nerves. "Yeah?"

"The word just came in. Thought you'd want to know."

Nick listened, his expression growing grimmer with every word. "Is that it?" he asked when Jackson stopped.

"Yeah, except for one thing. Do you need me out there?"

"No." Nick strode the length of the extension cord. Opening a dresser drawer, he took out his gun. "Thanks, but I can handle it. Talk to you later."

"You do that. I'll be waiting. Watch your back."

"I always do." Nick cradled the receiver, grabbed his shirt and stalked down the hall calling for Marcy, not surprised when she didn't answer. He stopped in the kitchen to get a flashlight, then turned to the door.

The open door.

He closed it behind him with a soft snick that did nothing to relieve his temper. He was going to have a talk with her, he promised himself, breaking into a ground-covering jog. A long talk. All about the purpose of fancy locks on doors and windows.

He took the steps leading to Zelda's porch three at a time and swung through the door.

Open, of course.

The house was empty. He knew it as soon as he stepped inside, but he made a rapid, thorough search of each room before he left.

Two houses unlocked and wide open, two women gone. Take it easy, Nick calmed himself, breaking into a lope down the quiet road. The situation would be more volatile and lethal in the city—any city—than it was in Joshua Junction. It could be worse, a lot worse. There was still time. He glanced at his watch. Plenty of time.

They hadn't been dragged out of the houses. There wasn't a trace of force. They had walked out, leaving the doors wide open behind them. Yeah, he decided grimly, he was going to talk to both of them about observing a few simple everyday precautions. Like closing windows and doors. And locking them. And carrying keys to open the locked doors. Basic stuff.

They were too damn curious for their own good. And trusting. They'd flit off to investigate haunted houses or chase ghosts with never a thought that they might run into trouble. Sure they were intelligent women, both of them. Bright as they came. He just wished they had a few street smarts as part of the package.

But maybe Marcy's instincts and Zelda's highly touted ESP would warn them if things started getting shaky. And God only knew it could, if anything at all went wrong tonight.

He crested the hill and crouched in the shadow of a scrub oak to look around, swearing absently as his knee twinged. It was getting better, but it still let him know when he pushed it too far. The three-quarter moon rode overhead, lighting the small valley, casting blocks of shadows around trees and clumps of bushes, but nothing moved. He picked up a small stone, absently tossing it into the air and catching it, waiting.

Nick stood motionless, scanning the area, looking for any movement in the shadows below. After another glance at his watch, he started down the hill. Between the dry brush and pebbles rolling underfoot, there was no quiet way to do it, so he made it fast.

At the bottom, he waited, listening. The yard was a combination of dead grass, hard dirt, a few tenacious cactus plants and scrawny bushes. Once he crossed it, it only took another minute to circle the house and Nick allowed himself the time, staying in the shadows and coming to a stop at the back porch.

"Hell."

He rubbed the back of his neck and swore as he looked down at the patch of scuffed dust at the base of the stairs. They might as well have left a neon arrow pointing inside, he thought in disgust. He looked up a notch higher and shook his head. He didn't need the flashlight to see the prints dug into the dust-covered wood. Two pairs of small tennis shoes tracked up the steps, around a soft spot in the center of the porch and up to the door.

The open door.

Exasperated, he rested his fists on his hips. When something bit into his palm, he opened his hand and realized he was still carrying the small rock he'd picked up on the hill. Tossing it aside, he watched it bounce and come to a stop with a clink against the basement window. The small sound seemed loud in the silence, and he turned back to the porch.

Silently, he followed their trail over the threshold and into the room. His hand touched the doorknob just as a raspy shriek erupted into the night air, splitting the silence with its shocking abandon.

"Help!" it wailed. *"Run, run, ruunnnn!"*

A shiver worked up Nick's spine at the inhuman wail. If that was what Marcy heard that night, no wonder she'd run, he thought grimly, closing the door quietly behind him. Even knowing—or suspecting—what it was, it came as a shock. Adrenaline was racing through his blood-stream like a freight train.

Nick took a steadying breath and flicked on the flashlight, keeping the beam close to the floor. He eased around the perimeter of the room, rather than walking across it, working his way to the door at the far end. He entered the next room, bouncing the light in all four corners. It was as large as the first and just as empty.

Where the hell are they?

He knew they were here. Somewhere. But where would two trusting and inventive women hell-bent on conducting a séance settle down to business?

He tried to put himself in their position—a trick that worked well enough for him when he was on the job—and realized that he couldn't. He could no more understand the workings of their minds than he could swallow one of the prickly pears out in the yard. They might as well be alien beings. Of course, he could just be out of touch. His work brought him closer to the scum of the world than the average, ordinary, decent citizen.

He shook his head and a wry grin twisted his lips as he skirted the room, keeping close to the walls. These two defied classification. They were decent, definitely. But average? No way. He coped with average pretty well, but these two had kept him off balance from the start. And ordinary? Zelda was in a class by herself, and Marcy O'Bannon of the Santa Barbara O'Bannons? If she was ordinary, then God help the men of the world.

Ordinary wasn't a valiant, free-spirit gift wrapped in a body custom-made for one particular man. *Ordinary* didn't have witch's eyes that teased and invited, or hair like dark fire that slid over a man like silken flames. *Ordinary* didn't have endless legs that wrapped around a man, holding him close and tight to a body that gave and took with equal pleasure and generosity.

No, ordinary was definitely not the— The thought vanished as he stepped into the dining room. Well, hell, he thought in disgust, looking at the open panel spilling light into the otherwise pitch-black room. Zelda, in one of her rambling monologues, had handed him the location on a silver platter and he had forgotten. Stoner, the great detective, had forgotten a secret room.

Silently pacing the length of the dining room, he forced himself to calm down. After all, he reminded himself, he didn't want to go rushing in there and scare them half to death. He wanted to deal with them in a reasonable, detached, professional manner.

Then he'd throttle them.

Nick drew to a halt outside the door. He blinked in disbelief, taking in the lace tablecloth, the fancy candlesticks on the mantel bathing the room in golden light, the crystal ball on the table and the quiet intensity of the women seated at the table.

He exhaled sharply and lifted his eyes to the ceiling, while rage washed over him. It was a natural reaction. He knew it. He also knew that he had been more afraid than he had admitted, even to himself. They were safe, he told himself, repeating it like a mantra. They were safe.

They were also crazy, rash and irresponsible. They had no right to risk their lives for a crazy adventure. They had no right to risk his sanity. They belonged under lock and key— preferably *his* lock and *his* key.

He reached for the panel door, planning to tell them exactly that when he heard the sound of a four-wheel drive laboring up the hill.

Marcy shifted restlessly on the cushion, wincing when it gave a squishy burping sound. "Zelda, how long are we going to sit here staring at that thing?"

"Until something happens."

"That could be hours." Or never. "What if nothing happens say . . . in a couple of hours?" she asked tactfully.

"We keep waiting."

Dropping tact, Marcy tried again. "We have a deadline, of sorts. If Nick wakes up and figures out where we are, he's going to come over here breathing fire. Can't you, uh, speed things up just a little?"

Zelda folded her hands on the table and inched closer to the crystal. "The spirits aren't governed by clocks," she explained patiently. "They make their presence known when it's appropriate."

"But—"

"Shhh! Let your mind drift and be receptive."

Receptive to what? Marcy wondered. Her mind was drifting, but she doubted her thoughts were conducive to peace and serenity. Nick was not going to be a happy camper if he woke up and found her gone again. He might be the sexiest man to ever come strolling down the pike, but he was definitely not the most easygoing, and she had a nasty feeling that when it got out of hand, his temper was formidable. She really didn't want to find out the hard way.

"Zelda, maybe you read the directions wrong or something. Maybe we should give it another day or so. Hmmm?" she asked finally. "What do you think?"

"Marcy!" Zelda hissed. "I think I'm beginning to see something! Just remember, whatever happens, we're protected by a white light. Don't be frightened."

On that encouraging note, Zelda scooted her chair closer to the table, focusing her entire attention on the crystal ball. The words had barely left her mouth when an unholy scream pierced the air.

"Run, run, ruunnn!"

Marcy jumped. Leaning forward, half fascinated, half appalled, she demanded, "Did you do that?"

Eyes sparkling with excitement, Zelda grinned. "I don't know," she admitted. "But I felt something before it happened."

"Felt what?"

"I don't know," she said again with a shrug. "A feeling of... it'll sound strange," she warned.

"What?"

"A gathering of power, a feeling of great anticipation. I knew something was going to happen."

Looking at the other woman with a new sense of respect, Marcy said slowly, "If you conjure up more of that, I don't think I want to be around."

Zelda gave her hand a comforting pat. "Remember, nothing can hurt you. You are—"

"I know, surrounded by white light. I think I'd rather have a big stick."

"Oh, ye of little faith." Zelda chuckled, obviously delighted with her success and hot to see what else she could do. "Marcy, I can't give up now. Please don't ask me to."

"I won't," she said slowly. "At least, not yet. But I'll be honest. I'm not nearly as thrilled with this as I thought I'd be. If it gets much more exciting, I'm dousing the candles and we're heading for home."

"Mmm," Zelda agreed in a preoccupied voice. "Whatever you say. Just don't talk to me until I get through, okay? When you do, it seems to short circuit something and I find it very distracting." She closed her eyes and took several deep breaths.

Short circuit? Marcy watched with growing concern as the muscles in Zelda's throat and face went slack. Her breathing fell into a noticeably slower rhythm and her brown eyes were unblinking, gazing at the crystal with a distant inward focus.

Fifteen minutes, she decided abruptly. That's the outside limit. I'll give her that much time, then short circuit or not, I'm getting her out of here. She sighed and leaned back in her chair, the burping cushion almost masking the soft sound behind her.

Almost, but not quite.

She turned her head just as Nick slid through the open panel, pulling it closed behind him.

Ten

———

"Nick! What are you doing here?" Marcy glanced guiltily at Zelda and lowered her voice. "You didn't have to come looking for us," she hissed. "We were leaving soon. Honest. In fifteen or twenty minutes."

"Well, you're not now." He cast an assessing glance around the cubicle and shook his head. "I sure hope you're not claustrophobic."

"What do you mean?"

"Your plans have just been changed," he said succinctly. Nodding toward the mantel, he added, "Douse the lights."

"*What?*" Marcy looked appalled. "And sit here in the dark with spiders and God only knows what else?"

"The lights. Out. Now!"

Marcy glared at him, prepared to argue the point, but what she saw in his face stopped her. Nick was furious. She had expected that, would have been astounded and, yes, a bit disappointed, if he hadn't been. But something was overriding his anger, an urgency, a grim purposefulness that made her blink and think of Nick the Cop on the job, tracking down the bad guys.

"How about half of them?" she offered.

"Marcy, it's not negotiable," he snapped, keeping his voice pitched low. "Do it!"

He hadn't moved away from the door, she noted absently. He stood half facing it, as if expecting trouble from someone or something on the other side; tilting his head, as if he were listening for a distant sound.

A shiver rippled up her spine. "What's the matter?"

Nick held up his hand in a silencing gesture. "Not now. The lights," he reminded her.

"Nick," she whispered to his back, "I'm not being stubborn. I honestly don't think I can sit here in the dark with spiders and..." Knowing how ridiculous it would sound, she stopped, her words dwindling away.

"And what?"

"And Zelda conjuring up spirits," she blurted, fully expecting him to laugh but beyond the point where she cared. "You should have seen what she did a while ago. At least," she amended conscientiously, "she *might* have done it. And if she comes up with anything else like that, I don't think I can—"

Nick pressed his forehead against the paneling and sighed. "All right," he interrupted with a growl, "one candle. *One.* When I was in the dining room, I couldn't see any light except what came through the open panel, so it should be safe."

"Okay." When Marcy jumped up to reach for one of the branched candlesticks, the cushion beneath her gave a raspy grumble. That didn't surprise her nearly as much as Nick's reaction did. She was blowing out the first candle when he swung around, a blur of coordination and coiled muscles. In one smooth movement he reached behind him, pivoted on the balls of his feet and crouched in a marksman's stance, a gun gripped between his outstretched hands, aimed straight at the chair—and Zelda.

"Nick!" Marcy's horrified whisper broke the charged silence. "What are you doing?"

With painful slowness the tension seeped out of him and he lowered the pistol, muttering a stark, succinct oath as he tucked it out of sight. Marcy shakily blew out four more candles and sagged against the wall. Long seconds later she drew in a ragged breath and moved closer to Nick, touching his arm with a soothing hand.

"I don't think she even noticed," she whispered. "It's all right." But the flame from the remaining candle cast enough light to convince her that it—whatever it was—was definitely not all right. The expression in Nick's eyes was as flinty as his face. He looked like a man who had withdrawn from all tenderness, all warmth. Like a man who faced the world alone, and the look chilled Marcy right down to her bones. Her hand fell to her side when he moved away from her touch.

"What's the matter with her?" Nick's bleak gaze settled on Zelda.

"I think she's in a trance."

"Terrific."

Zelda took a deep breath, the sound loud in the small room, startling the two of them. She held the air deep in her lungs and slowly exhaled through her nose. "I feel your presence," she murmured with closed eyes. "You are most welcome. Gray Feather extends his greetings and so do I. If you have anything to say—"

Nick scowled. "Thank you," he said with biting sarcasm. "It's nice that you'll listen after getting me out of bed in the middle—"

"Uh, Nick." Marcy squeezed his arm. "I don't think she's talking to you."

He gazed around the minuscule room, checking all four corners with elaborate patience. "I sure don't see anyone else."

"That's the point." She gazed around, a skittish look in her green eyes. "I think she's convening the spirits, or whatever you call it."

"Oh, hell." He cast a frustrated look at the older woman. Zelda sat with her hands on the table, palms up, fingers slightly curved, her face serene and composed. "That's all we need. Not that I think for a minute that she can do it, but—" He glanced again at the table, his gaze pinned on the crystal ball. "Good God!" He sounded revolted. "She actually has one."

"You thought she was kidding?"

"I hoped so. That settles it. We're not going to spend the rest of the night listening to her talk to imaginary spooks. I'm going to wake her up."

"No!" Marcy grabbed at his shirt. "Don't touch her."

"Why not?"

Marcy shook her head slowly. "I just don't think you should. She told me it jarred her when people talked to her. I have a feeling that shaking her would even be worse."

"Look, if she's so sensitive and good at picking up vibes, she'd get mine and run screaming out of the room. Believe me, there's enough hostility packed in them to—"

"Give us a sign," Zelda murmured. "Let us know that you are here with us."

Nick ran a harried hand through his hair. "Don't let her get started," he warned.

Whatever else he had to say on the subject was lost when a crash resounded through the house, making the whole place shudder.

Marcy's eyes widened and she grabbed for her notebook. She stared at Zelda in amazement, then turned to Nick. "Do you think—"

Nick swore and pulled her close. Keeping his voice below the level of a whisper, he warned, "Not another word, Marcy. Promise me, until I say it's safe." When she just stared at him, his hand tightened on her arm. "I mean it. Not...a...word. Promise me." She nodded slowly, and he relaxed his grip. "And try to keep her quiet." He tilted his head toward Zelda. When she gave him a helpless what-can-I-do? shrug, he agreed, but still nudged her closer to the other woman, keeping her away from the door.

Marcy quietly returned to her chair, sliding her hands across the table until they brushed against Zelda's. From the corner of her eye she saw Nick move one of the wooden chairs away from the wall and straddle it. His arms, braced across the back, pointed directly at the door.

Between his hands, also pointing directly at the door, was his gun.

The slight quiver of tension in Zelda's hands alerted her, but before Marcy could react, Zelda parted her lips. "Lift up your voices," she crooned softly. "Those of you who want to speak, let us know."

Marcy threw Nick a helpless glance, but although he flinched, he didn't turn his attention from the door.

"Whenever you like," Zelda said, her voice soothing. "We're ready."

Apparently, so were the spirits, Marcy thought in wide-eyed astonishment, because a veritable cacophony of sound filled the room.

Unintelligible commands, sounding magnified and stilted resounded through the house.

"Help!" screeched an abrasive voice that had all the resonance of fingernails scratching on a blackboard.

"Run, run, ruunnn!" shrieked another.

"Silencio!" shrilled a third.

Marcy scribbled in her notebook, stopping to look up only when Zelda sighed. The older woman's eyes were open, filled with exaltation and nonplussed excitement.

"Signs," Zelda murmured with deep satisfaction. "Show me a sign, I said, and just look what—"

Rapid footsteps interrupted her, pounding through the house from front to back and then reversing the procedure.

Zelda blinked. "My goodness. I wasn't even trying that time. All I have to do is—"

"Don't!" Marcy whispered. "Don't say another word. If you're doing this, you've stirred up enough spirits to keep things hopping for a month."

When Marcy awoke, it was late afternoon. She stretched and groaned, looking around the room. She was in her own bed, the pillow next to hers smooth and untouched. Her pang of disappointment was...unsettling. And surprising. Two weeks ago she hadn't even known that Nick Stoner existed, and now if she woke up without his arms around her she felt bereft.

She had slept in her room, certain that Nick would join her during the night. Obviously, he hadn't. More than likely because he was still angry. Folding her hands behind her head and staring up at the fan, she reflected for a moment. Angry wasn't the word for his mood last night. Furious was closer.

Or enraged.

Last night...

If she lived to be a very old lady, the image of Nick facing the door, gun in hand, was one she would never forget. He had remained that way for several hours, hardly blinking, silent and withdrawn, yet with a grimness that told her more clearly than words what would happen if anyone or anything opened the door: he would squeeze the trigger and shoot.

The door had not been touched and, finally, long after the last mysterious sound had died away, he had moved. Still silent, he reached for the candle and searched around the panel door until he located the release. With a glance that kept them rooted to their chairs, he'd slid open the panel and disappeared. Several minutes later, he'd returned, stuffed Zelda's apparatus in the pack and gestured for them to follow him.

Marcy grimaced at the memory. Thoroughly cowed by that time, she and Zelda had followed. All the way home. Without a word— especially about the fact that he was limping again. When they got back to the house, he had said in a distant voice that she must be tired. She was, and had gone to her own bed and slept for almost twelve hours. She didn't count the time as wasted. Between making love with Nick for hours on end and being terrorized in a haunted house, she figured she deserved it.

Throwing back the sheet, Marcy reflected that it was time to make her peace with Nick. With any luck at all he'd be rested and in a better mood. But first things first, she decided, swinging her feet to the floor. She needed a shower and some food before she tackled him.

Thirty minutes later she headed for the kitchen, following the aroma of broiling steak. Breezing through the door, she said lightly, "Did I luck out, or what? There's no end to your talents. Handyman, bodyguard, cook, what I call a real Renaissance m—" She stopped in midword, staring at the figure swathed in a huge white apron. For once, the gauzy dress fabric was sternly controlled, and a number of slim bracelets were piled haphazardly on the windowsill.

"Zelda! What on earth are you doing here?"

"Cooking," the older woman replied literally, sparing her a quick look. "I thought you'd be hungry."

"I am. Starved, as a matter of fact. But why are you here? Where's Nick?"

Zelda peered into the broiler. "How do you like your steak?"

"Pink, but definitely not mooing." Marcy looked around. "Where's Nick?" she repeated patiently.

"The dear boy's been very busy today, what with talking to the officers who conducted the raid last night."

"Raid?"

Zelda nodded, staring indecisively at the steaks.

"What raid? And by who? Whom?"

"By the U.S. Fish and Wildlife Service, according to what Nick learned from one of his friends. They were cracking down on a gang smuggling rare and endangered parrots in from Mexico and Latin America."

"I don't believe it," Marcy said, stunned. "I mean, I do believe it if you say so, but—Parrots?" she asked with a dawning grin. *"Parrots?"*

Zelda sighed. "Parrots. And I was so sure— But Nick said there was no mistake. Not all of them were wild, of course. Some belonged to the smugglers and had been taught to say a few words."

"Like *run* and *help?*" Marcy asked, repeating the wailing words that had sounded so terrifying in the still of the night.

"Uh-huh." Zelda nodded as she removed two spitting steaks from the fire. "Apparently the smugglers had a limited English vocabulary or a skewed sense of humor. Or they thought the words appropriate for a house that looked haunted. They told the officers that they left some of the trained parrots along with the ones that were for sale in the basement of the Mulroony place to scare people off with their cries.''

"Well, they—the parrots, I mean—certainly earned their birdseed or whatever they eat. They scared the doodah out of me.'' Marcy watched as Zelda poured some steaming carrots into a bowl. "I can't understand why we're the only ones who heard the birds. None of the people I talked to in town ever mentioned any unusual noises.''

Zelda clattered pans briskly at the sink. "I think we're the only ones who went out there. Most of the people have lived around here too long to be interested in the old place. And they go to bed with the chickens.'' She shrugged. "Not many people around here go strolling after midnight.''

"Or are nosy enough to poke around old, abandoned buildings?''

"Uh-huh.''

"What about the howling dogs?'' Marcy asked, reluctant to give up on the Indian who celebrated centennials. She had gotten rather fond of him.

Zelda sighed. "Nick believes that they were disturbed by the vehicles coming in late at night.''

"The man has absolutely no imagination,'' Marcy muttered, putting silver and two cups on the glass table. "So there's no ghost,'' she finally asked, breaking the thoughtful silence that had fallen between them.

Zelda looked up at her for a long moment, then busied herself carrying food to the table. "So the dear boy says.''

Ha, Marcy thought with a grin. She hasn't given up. "Speaking of our favorite cop," she said casually. "Where is he? I've never known him to miss a meal."

Zelda waved Marcy to a seat and settled in a chair across from her. "Gray Feather told me to continue my studies with the crystal ball. I was using it for meditation this morning when I had a brilliant idea, and I knew I had to discuss it with you."

Marcy dropped her fork. "No. Absolutely not."

"What?"

"I will not do another séance. I don't know how much you had to do with what happened last night, if anything, but I'm not going through that again. If you do it again, you're on your own."

"We'll talk about it later," Zelda said placidly. "Gray Feather *said* we would." Changing the subject abruptly, she said, "Perhaps my imagination did carry me away. With our Indian ghost, I mean. What are you going to do? Will your editor mind?"

"Sure he'll mind, but it comes with the territory. I can't invent one." Marcy lifted her glass of ice water and pressed it on the tabletop, making a series of transparent, interlocking rings. Eyeing them thoughtfully, she said, "You know, handled the right way, the incident could make a pretty entertaining story."

"I suppose," Zelda agreed vaguely, already preoccupied with her own thoughts.

"I'll think about it. I wonder how Nick would like being featured in a story. With another name, of course. You know, one of those name-changed-to-protect-the-innocent stories." A yawn overtook Marcy. Stretching luxuriously, she said, "Now, for the third or fourth time, where is our resident fuzz?"

Zelda moved aside her plate and rested her lightly clasped hands on the glass table. "Marcy," she began, not lifting her gaze from her plump fingers, "Gray Feather said it's very important that you understand something."

Marcy sighed.

"At any given time, we are all exactly where we are supposed to be."

Marcy waited. When Zelda said nothing more, she finally asked, "That's it? That's the message?"

Zelda nodded.

"He's a bit inscrutable, isn't he? Well, I'll take him at face value for the moment. I'm here, you're there, and Cristobel is still in Alaska. Now where the heck is Nick?"

Zelda thrust her head in the capacious pocket of the apron. She pulled out a small white envelope and handed it to Marcy. "He asked me to give you this."

She knew what it said before she reached across the table to take it. She also realized that, unconsciously, she had been expecting it. It had just happened sooner than she'd expected. "He's gone, isn't he?"

Zelda nodded slowly, watching Marcy with serene eyes. "Yes. To his condo. Once he knew that we were all right and talked to his friends about the raid, he said his leg was fine now, gave me another note for Cristobel and left." She blinked and said earnestly, "You *must* remember Gray Feather's message. Of course, you love him. Nick, I mean."

"Of course," Marcy agreed numbly, opening the envelope. The message, written in his bold scrawl, was brief.

Marcy,
I'm sorry to do it like this, but it's the best way. I won't have you hurt because of me. Ever. Be happy.
                                        Nick

She tossed the note on the table, blinking back tears. "The fool! The idiotic, blasted fool!"

"People in love have a way of complicating their lives. Unnecessarily, of course. What are you going to do?"

"I don't know."

"When the time is right, you will." Zelda cleared her throat. "Just as I know that I'm ready to take another step. Now, Marcy, I know that you're upset, and it may be selfish of me to discuss my plans with you at this time, but Gray Feather said it is the *right* time. It's very important."

Marcy listened, eventually torn between astonishment and amusement. And for a few minutes she managed to forget Nick's note.

Later that evening, after Zelda had returned home, presumably to communicate with her crystal ball, Marcy gazed at the crumpled letter. She had reread it more times than she cared to count. Once, she had wadded it up and thrown it in the trash, only to retrieve it a few minutes later.

Who the hell did he think he was? Fury rode her as she paced the living room. The fact that the room was full of memories didn't help matters. She skirted the window where he had stood looking down at her in the moonlit yard, eventually pulling her up into his arms. And the couch where he had held her after the storm—before he carried her to his bed.

How could he just cut it off? Walk away without even trying?

And that was the crux of the matter, she admitted silently. It was easier to deal with anger than the pain that seeped through to her bones. Didn't he care enough? As much as she did? She dropped into a chair and stared blindly at the wall.

I won't have you hurt because of me. Ever.

Long minutes later, she blinked, remembering what Zelda had said about lovers complicating their lives.

Of course, Nick cared. Too much. She had the good—and bad—fortune to be in love with a noble man. One who was determined to protect her—from both him and herself. He wasn't going to let her get hurt by marrying a cop or having a relationship with one. He assumed that he knew what was best for her.

He assumed wrong.

So what was she going to do? Zelda had also said that when the time was right, she would know.

For once, Zelda was right.

She was going to change his mind. But first, she had to get his attention. Once she did that, everything would work out.

All right, it was over. Finished. Done. It wasn't the end of the world. Nick shifted uncomfortably on the lounge chair, taking his rotten temper out on the huge man lounging beside him, telling himself it was because his knee was still aching.

"You did the right thing," Jackson said lazily. "Walk out before a woman gets too serious. Any woman. In our line of work, it's the only way."

Only it wasn't *any* woman. It was Marcy. Marcy O'Bannon of the Santa Barbara O'Bannons. A sprite. Funny, beautiful, maddening Marcy. With hair like silken fire, designed to drive a man mad. He should be relieved. He *was* relieved. He didn't have to worry about where she was anymore. No more waking up in the middle of the night and finding her gone. No more gut-wrenching fear, no more aging ten years in ten minutes because of one of her hair-raising schemes.

No more Marcy O'Bannon. Period.

Yeah, he felt great. Just great.

"If I knew you had a view like this, I would've been here sooner," Jackson murmured. "Will you *look* at that."

Nick kept his eyes closed. None of his views had red hair and green eyes, so he wasn't interested.

"And she's friendly." Jackson's voice was almost reverent. "She's coming over."

"Hi, guys. This seat taken?"

Nick gripped the arms of the lounge, his heart beating so fast he could barely hear the pounding in his ears.

"I'm Marcy O'Bannon. You must be Jackson, the friendly one of the deadly duo."

"What makes you say that?" He could hear the grin in Jackson's voice.

"Nick's too grim. If you guys play good cop, bad cop, *you* have to be the one in the white hat. He'd scare people to death."

Jackson chuckled. "You're right. I'm friendly. Very friendly. In fact, if you'd like to go somewhere and find out how friendly—"

"Like hell she will." Nick opened his eyes and stared menacingly at his grinning partner. His grim gaze switched to Marcy. "What are you doing here?"

"Working. Starting tomorrow. After I get my hair cut."

"Like hell you will!"

She dropped into a chair next to Jackson, smiling at the blond giant. "You are a big one, aren't you?" She tilted her head. "Handsome, too. Nick didn't tell me that part."

"You mean he even mentioned me?"

"You're not going to cut your hair," Nick said between clenched teeth.

Marcy touched Jackson's arm. "Now and again."

"Where?" Nick demanded, eyeing her too-short shorts and too-snug shirt with a frown. Jackson sprawled back in his chair, wearing a dark swimsuit that didn't cover a hell of a lot. That it was a twin to his own suit was immaterial.

"Where, what?"

"Where are you working?"

"Here in town. Chasing more ghosts." Marcy raised her face to the sun.

"What do you mean, more?"

"You have a point," she conceded. "The first one fizzled. No ghost, no ghost story."

Jackson covered her hand with his. "That's too bad. Nick told me about it."

"Ah, well." Marcy gave a philosophical chuckle. "It wasn't all for naught. My editor said he'd settle for a humorous piece about an intrepid ghost buster who finds a clutch of parrots instead."

Nick narrowed his eyes, his gaze settling on his partner's large hand. "Don't you have something you have to do? Somewhere else?"

"Nope." Jackson settled deeper into the chair. "I'm just gonna sit here in the sun and soak up the rays."

"I hear Curtis is turning in his pipe for cigars," Nick said idly. "It's gonna be rough working with him. Especially if I have to ask for a couple more weeks of sick leave."

"Low blow, partner. On second thought—" Jackson shot to his feet "—it was nice meeting you, Marcy." He smiled down at her, reluctantly returning her hand. "Hope I see you again."

"That was rude and uncalled for," Marcy told Nick, shooting him a severe frown as Jackson headed for his car.

"Yeah, it was, wasn't it?" he said complacently, closing his eyes again. "How's Zelda doing?"

"She's resilient. She bounced right back. In fact, she's got a new plan up her sleeve. A real doozy." Marcy kicked off her sandals and quietly slid out of her shorts and top, leaning back with a sigh.

Nick grinned. "I bet she does. Who's the poor sucker she's going to steamroll this time?"

"You."

Nick stiffened. He didn't have to look at Marcy to see that she was telling the truth. He could hear the amusement in her voice. And the satisfaction.

"What do you mean, me?"

"You're the lucky one, Stoner. She could have chosen any man in the world, but she wanted rock-solid Nick Stoner."

"For what?" he asked with foreboding.

"To work with." She couldn't contain the ripple of laughter. "She decided she wants to help the police on their tough cases, and since Joshua Junction doesn't get much excitement, she's willing to travel to San Diego. But she told your captain that she only wants to work with you."

"*Told?*"

"Yesterday," she said gently.

"Oh, my God."

"He said he'd get back to her," Marcy added helpfully.

Nick swung around to face her, his look of undiluted horror changing to no expression at all. "What is that thing you almost have on?" he demanded quietly.

Marcy's heart dropped. For an awful moment she thought she had failed. He didn't sound like a man who cared one way or another what she wore. Then she saw the anger in his dark eyes and the muscle bunching in his cheek.

"What, this?" She waved her hand, gesturing toward the most outrageously skimpy assortment of spaghetti straps and minuscule patches of fabric that she had ever seen. It had taken courage to buy it and almost more courage than she'd had that morning to put it on.

Before she could lose her nerve, she stood, turning in place like a model. "What do you think, is it me?"

"Put . . . your . . . clothes . . . on."

Nick's voice was so low it barely carried the short distance between them. Marcy swallowed. He didn't sound amused. But then it hadn't been her plan to entertain him. She wanted him so mad he couldn't see straight.

She snatched up her clothes from the chair beside her and held them up. "You mean these?" Before he could reply, the shorts and top slipped from her fingers and fell into the pool.

"Oops." Marcy stared in genuine dismay at the slowly sinking clothes. Even though she had done it intentionally, she had nothing else with her. If Nick sent her away, it was going to be a long walk back to the car. "I'll get them."

Nick shot to his feet. "Don't!"

"What? They're sinking." She started to lean forward.

"Don't—bend over. Don't move. I'll get them." His lean body hit the water in a shallow dive. Seconds later he surfaced, braced his hands on the side of the pool and surged out of the water to stand beside her. One wet hand clamped around her arm. "Come on."

Marcy dug in her heels. "Where?"

Nick shook his hair back off his face, his dark eyes blazing. "My place, where do you think?"

He hustled her up the stairs and dropped her arm as soon as they were through the door. "I'll put these in the dryer," he said, turning away.

"No!" Marcy grabbed his wrist. "You can't. They'll shrink. They're supposed to drip dry."

He gave her a grim look and left the room. When he came back, he had a blue long-sleeved shirt in his hands. Holding it, he said, "Here, put it on."

She slid her arms into the sleeves and began rolling up the cuffs. The hem almost reached her knees. Her breath almost stopped when his fingers brushed her nape, easing her hair out from beneath the collar and smoothing it over her shoulders, almost as if he couldn't keep his hands away from it, she thought with a spark of hope.

He stepped back and she swung around, her hair billowing out like a fiery banner. He hadn't taken time to dry off and beads of water clung to his tan flesh. Several drops ran down his chest, trailing down the narrow line of dark hair and soaking into his suit. But his hair didn't end there. She remembered all too clearly tracing it down to a denser thatch that—

"Why did you come?"

"Why did you leave?" Marcy's anger overrode the pain in his voice.

"Because I'm no good for you."

"Oh, you decided that all by yourself. Did you ever think of asking me what *I* thought?"

"No." His voice hardened. "Because you're too soft—"

"Soft."

"Too compassionate. Too much like Cristobel. Hell, she wanted to mother a mugger and almost got stabbed for her efforts. You wouldn't think twice about tackling a hard-nosed cop who sees more ugliness in one day than you've probably seen in a lifetime. After a while, you don't walk away from the stuff, Marcy, it gets to be a part of you. And I don't want it touching you."

"*Soft?*" she repeated in a disbelieving voice. "Let me tell you about soft, Stoner." She poked a finger in his chest and jabbed with almost every word. "From the beginning of time women have mated with warriors and watched them go to battle. They feared for them while they were gone and rejoiced when they returned. They had their babies and raised their children. They grieved when their men didn't make it back, but by God they didn't curl up their toes and give up, or else civilization as we know it would have ended before it began. So you can talk to me about a lot of things, but not...about...*soft!*"

She ended with a final thump on his chest and whirled away, standing at the window, looking down on the pool, trying and failing to rein in her temper.

Nick looked at her elegant, infuriated back and almost choked with pride. She looked like an enraged canary taking on a pit bull. She was outweighed, outranked and outsized, but would she back down, even an inch? Hell, no! She was fighting for him, for them, and she wasn't about to let up.

But he couldn't let her win this battle, because if she did, for the rest of her life, she lost. And he couldn't let that happen. Not to Marcy.

"I saw your expression the other night when I pulled out my gun." His voice was bleak. "I knew then what I had been telling myself all along. It would never work."

Marcy spun around, barely containing her anger and fear. "And what did my expression say?"

"You were disgusted. And scared. You sat there in that yellow sweatshirt, looking like a beam of sunlight that was trying to brighten the world. And you were surrounded by—"

"I hope you're better at your job than you are at reading a woman, Stoner," Marcy said briskly, her heart almost breaking at the look on his face. He had so much love to give and he didn't even seem to know it. He needed love and he was determined to toss it away, just to save her. From him. The idiot, she thought with utter exasperation.

"Outside of TV and the movies, I'd never even seen a gun—much less someone pointing one at another person. And scared? Sure I was scared. By that time, I didn't know *what* was outside the door. But you know what, Stoner? You planted yourself—along with that trusty gun of yours—right between me and it. Whatever it was out there in the darkness had to come through the door and climb over you before it got to me. And you know what? I knew it was never going to do that."

She covered the distance between them and wrapped her arms around his lean waist, lifting her face to his. "I love you, Nick Stoner," she whispered, touching her lips to his chest. "And I learned something while we waited in that little room the other night."

Nick groaned. Her nipples were beaded and tight, nudging him with every rapid breath she took. "What?" He cleared his throat. "What did you learn?"

Her smile was small and very feminine. "That 'serve and protect' wasn't just part of a motto for you. It's in your bones and blood. You'll always take care of what belongs to you. And that means me. I know, too, that as hard as you worked to keep the darkness out of that room, you would never bring it home with you. You will never let it touch me."

She stepped back, her eyes meeting his. "Look at me, Nick." She slipped out of his shirt and stood there a long moment before she reached up to undo the straps of her bikini. "I'm a woman, but I'm not soft and I'm not weak. The only way you're going to get rid of me is to tell me that you don't love me."

It was the hardest thing he ever did, but he tried. "Marcy—"

The top slid to the floor, baring her breasts. "All you have to say is 'I don't love you.'"

"For God's sake—"

The bottom joined the other piece on the floor, and an exultant smile lit her face. "If you can't, then you have me for life."

"I don't—"

Before he could finish, shock hit her, wiping away the smile, leaving a look of sick dismay in her eyes. Her hands, which had begun to twine around his neck, retreated in an ageless gesture of vulnerable women, one covering her breasts, one moving lower.

"—just love you, Marcy. I'm crazy about you." Nick snatched her up in his arms and headed for the bedroom. "I can't live without you and I don't intend to try. Not anymore." He lifted her higher in his arms and touched his lips to the tip of her breast. "You've had your last chance, lady. You win. I'm tired of trying to be a hero. I'm not going through that again, ever, so you better mean what you just said. You're stuck with me, sweetheart. For a lifetime."

He tossed her lightly on the bed, shed his suit and followed her down. His fingers threaded through her hair, his hands shaping her skull, holding her still for his kiss. When he lifted his head, they were both breathing fast.

"Say it again," he ordered, parting her legs with his knee and fitting his hard body to her softer one.

"I love you." She kissed his chin, which was all she could reach. "I love you."

"Why did you wait so long?"

Marcy ran her hands along his shoulders, stroking the hair at his nape with gentle fingers. "It was only four days."

"It was hell."

Her fingers tightened, and his eyes met hers. "I wanted you to miss me," she whispered.

"I started doing that the minute I walked out Cristobel's door." He blinked down at her, a sexy pirate grin lighting his face. "Does she know where you are?"

She nodded. "When she got home, I told her all about us. Who do you think picked out the bathing suit?"

He groaned. "I didn't stand a chance."

"You love it." Marcy prodded his shoulder, and he obligingly rolled over, taking her with him. She sat up, settling her knees near his hips. Bracing her hands on his shoulders, she bent her head, watching her hair flow over his chest, loving the look of hunger in his dark eyes. "Admit it, Stoner," she ordered, pressing her knees together. "You love it."

"I love it. I love you." And he did. God, how he loved her. His hands slid up her thighs to mold her hips. "You're not going to cut your hair." It was half question, half command.

Marcy grinned down at him. "I was just trying to get your attention."

"You have my full and undivided attention," he said through clenched teeth, surging beneath her.

"Is *that* what that is?" Teasing green eyes widened when he gripped her hips and eased her down on him. "Oh, Nick."

He touched her gently, shuddering when shock jolted through her. "I can't wait, babe. Say it, please."

"I love you, Nick."

"For always."

She gasped. "I love you."

"Forever."

"I love— Oh!" Marcy arched her back, frantically grasping his thighs with her hands.

"You're all right, sweetheart. I've got you."

"Nick! *Nick!*"

Her cry shattered his control and he felt his life and love, the very essence of him, the very best of him, flowing into her.

Later, stretched out beside him, Marcy burrowed her head in the hollow of his shoulder. "I have a temper," she admitted.

"No!" Nick looked shocked. "Really?"

"We'll fight."

"And make up."

"You'll drive me crazy trying to protect me."

His arm tightened around her. "Damned straight, lady. I'm your full-time bodyguard for the next fifty or sixty years."

"You're not always going to like my work."

"No doubt I'll tell you when I don't."

She tilted her head to look up at him. "You're a hard man, Stoner."

He grinned and nudged her hip. "Yeah. I am."

Marcy gazed at him with love-drenched eyes. Her smile was the small, satisfied smile women have given men since time began.

She had his full attention now, and yes, everything would work out just fine.

*   *   *   *   *

SILHOUETTE® Desire®

THEY'RE HOT...
THEY'RE COOL...
THEY'RE ALL-AMERICAN GUYS...
THEY'RE RED, WHITE AND BLUE HEROES

Zeke #793 by Annette Broadrick *(Man of the Month)*
Ben #794 by Karen Leabo
Derek #795 by Leslie Davis Guccione
Cameron #796 by Beverly Barton
Jake #797 by Helen R. Myers
Will #798 by Kelly Jamison

Look for these six red-blooded, white-knight, blue-collar men
Coming your way next month
Only from Silhouette Desire

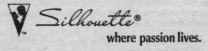

MEN MADE IN AMERICA

Fifty red-blooded, white-hot, true-blue hunks from every State in the Union!

Beginning in May, look for MEN MADE IN AMERICA! Written by some of our most popular authors, these stories feature fifty of the strongest, sexiest men, each from a different state in the union!

Two titles available every other month at your favorite retail outlet.

In July, look for:

CALL IT DESTINY by Jayne Ann Krentz (Arizona)
ANOTHER KIND OF LOVE by Mary Lynn Baxter (Arkansas)

In September, look for:

DECEPTIONS by Annette Broadrick (California)
STORMWALKER by Dallas Schulze (Colorado)

You won't be able to resist MEN MADE IN AMERICA!